Don't look at his eyes

Trisha quickly glanced to her boss's hair—those dark, wavy curls that she'd threaded her fingers through on a number of imaginary occasions.

Hair, bad.

She shot her gaze down to his chest.

Oh no, not the chest.

His ear. She could focus on his ear, she thought, before remembering she'd nibbled on it in cyberspace last Tuesday.

As her eyes scanned Logan's fine features like a pinball darting from one cushioned side to another, she realized she was sinking fast with no net.

She focused on the bronze Remington statue on the credenza behind him. *How fitting.* A team of wild horses. *'Cause it would take a team of wild horses to jolt the lust from my brain.*

Blaze™

Dear Reader,

That you're holding this book in your hand is a dream come true for me. It's my very first published novel, and hopefully the first of many more to come.

It's a pleasure to be able to share the story of Trisha and Logan. The idea came to me as I was reading a piece about an anonymous cybersex affair. I couldn't help but wonder what would happen if a person unwittingly spilled their darkest fantasies to someone they ended up knowing. Someone horrible, like a next-door neighbor, or worse—their boss!

Needless to say, I'd barely dropped the article on the coffee table before the plot for *Private Confessions* had completely unfolded in my mind, and I have to say, writing it was truly a blast.

I hope you enjoy the drama, the surprises, the laughs and yes, the romance. Please drop me a note and tell me what you think of it.

Happy reading!

Lori Borrill

PRIVATE CONFESSIONS

Lori Borrill

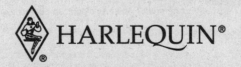

HARLEQUIN®

TORONTO • NEW YORK • LONDON
AMSTERDAM • PARIS • SYDNEY • HAMBURG
STOCKHOLM • ATHENS • TOKYO • MILAN • MADRID
PRAGUE • WARSAW • BUDAPEST • AUCKLAND

ISBN-13: 978-0-373-79312-9
ISBN-10:   0-373-79312-X

PRIVATE CONFESSIONS

ABOUT THE AUTHOR

An Oregon native, Lori Borrill moved to the Bay Area just out of high school and has been a transplant Californian ever since. Her weekdays are spent at the insurance company where she's been employed for over twenty years, and she credits her writing career to the unending help and support she receives from her husband and real-life hero. When not sitting in front of a computer, she can usually be found at the Little League fields playing proud parent to their son. She'd love to hear from readers, and can be reached through her Web site at www.LoriBorrill.com or via mail addressed to Harlequin Enterprises Ltd., 225 Duncan Mill Road, Toronto, Ontario M3B 3K9, Canada.

1

"YOU'RE WEARING a navy-blue skirt. It's tasteful. The hem stops just above the knee. Very professional on the outside, but I know you're naked underneath. You enjoy the silky feel of the fabric against your skin, don't you, Scorpio?"

Trisha Bain gulped as she read the words on her computer screen.

"I do," she typed, then hit Send.

"You step into my office and close the door behind you. Those gorgeous lips curve into a smile that makes everything else disappear. You lean against the door and look at me with those big blue eyes, eyes that reveal your innermost thoughts. Today, your eyes tell me you want me.

"Do you want me, Scorpio?"

"Yes," she typed. *Oh, yes.*

"I want you, too, baby. I've always wanted you."

She shivered.

"I pat my hand on the desk and you stroll over, swaying those hips that have been driving me crazy since the day we met. You're taking your time, teasing me, making me wait.

"You prop up on my desk and lift your feet to the

arms of my chair, spreading those long, sexy legs for me. So many times, I've wanted to reach out and touch them. Can I touch them, Scorpio?"

"Please," she typed.

"I place my hands on your ankles and slide my fingers up to your thighs. Your skin is smooth. I always knew it would be. I've been waiting for you. All day, I've been waiting for our meeting, watching the hours tick by. I can feel you trembling. You've been waiting, too, haven't you?"

"Yes," she typed, noticing how even the word looked breathy on the screen.

"I brush my fingers through your curls and groan when I feel the heat between your legs. You're wet. You've been thinking about me. Your scent is driving me to the edge and I can't resist a taste."

Oh, my.

"I slide my tongue over you and glide it around in circles. You like that, don't you, Scorpio?"

A bead of sweat moistened her upper lip and she squirmed as the sensation tingled in her most sensitive spot.

"Yes," she typed.

"You're so slick, so ready. Your breath goes heavy and you tilt your head back, thrusting your breasts in the air. I raise my eyes and watch them as they rise and fall with each breath you take, slowly at first then faster as the pressure builds.

"Your nipples pierce your shirt and their hardness fills me with need. You're about to slide over the edge. You want to go over, don't you?"

Trisha's hands trembled. Her toes curled inside her fuzzy blue slippers. Pisces was coming on strong tonight, and after a busy day at the agency, she could use the extra heat.

With fingers stiff and shaken, she forced them to the keyboard and typed, "Yes."

"It's better if I tease you."

Oh, no, don't tease.

"My tongue is barely touching you. You arch your back and pull yourself toward me, whimpering, begging for more. You try to get closer, but I dig my fingers in your thighs and hold you steady, making you wait. Your sex is so plump, so ready. You ache for me to move to that spot, that special place I know so well. Through long, ragged breaths, I hear you whisper, 'Please.' You want that spot, don't you?"

"Please," she typed, barely able to move her fingers over the keyboard. She swallowed hard, her body pulsed. She ached to be touched, but she knew Pisces47 was far from the end.

"Here's the spot, sweetheart, the spot that sends you over. My tongue slides along it with light, quick strokes, then harder, faster, until you burst in my mouth. You want to scream, but you've got to be quiet. People might hear. You bite your lip and hold your groan as the climax takes you.

"You quiver against my tongue. It feels so good, baby. I'm so hard for you. Every cell in my body cries to get inside, now, while you're still clamped tight. I need to take you in my arms, feel those sexy breasts against my chest and plunge inside until you beg for me to come."

Trisha's mouth went dry. She shifted in her seat, trying to relieve the pressure that swelled between her thighs. She wanted to reach down and relieve the throbbing, but it wasn't time. She needed Pisces inside.

"Can I take you now, Scorpio?"

With lightning-quick strokes, she typed, "Yes."

"I rise from my chair. You're open for me, so beautiful. Your eyes are heavy and sated, but the bulge between my legs starts the climb all over again."

She clasped her hands to the chair and held the breath in her lungs, unable to move until she saw what happened next.

"I unzip my trousers and you gasp at my length."

She gasped.

"I hold it at your entrance, brushing the tip against you, teasing you, swelling your already throbbing clit. You bite down on your lip some more and wait as your eyes plead for me to enter. You're ready for me, aren't you, Scorpio?"

She raised her hands to the keyboard. "Please," she typed, amazed by the quickness of her fingers.

"I slide my hands up under your skirt and place them on your hips, holding you firmly. My hands are hot to the touch. You feel me probing at your entrance and your breath comes out in pants. You're waiting, aching for the moment when I drive my shaft inside."

She dropped her hands from the keyboard and clasped them to the chair, digging her fingers into the rough woven fabric of the cushion. It was almost time, the pressure was nearly unbearable.

"In one quick stroke, I thrust inside and you clamp your jaw shut, holding the groan in your throat."

She sucked in a sharp breath and closed her eyes to seal the image in her mind. It was time to give Pisces full control. Sliding a hand between her thighs, she began a slow stroke.

"I'm big, harder than I've ever been before, and you're still tight from the climax. Your eyes roll back and close as a quick breath escapes your chest. Your smile tells me you like it. You need more. We've both wanted this for so long."

Forever, she thought as she swept her finger between her folds.

"I clasp my hands to your spine and push deeper while I nibble at your neck. You're salty from sweat. You smell like lavender. It's turning me on and I have to go deeper."

Yes.

"I fill you in one final thrust. You're so tight and slick. Your groan tells me I've found that spot and I begin to stroke as another climax builds."

Trisha gulped in air as she formed an image from the words on the screen. The room was hot, her breath shortened as she neared the edge of climax.

"My heart's beating fast. You place your hands on my chest. It's hard, damp and hot. You feel me growing inside. I'm about to lose control, Scorpio. You feel good, baby, and I need it all. I need to feel every inch of your body against mine. I thrust deeper and sink my face in the warm curve of your neck. And while I'm stroking inside you, you tell me your dreams."

My dreams?

"What are your dreams, Scorpio?"

Trisha stared at the words on the screen. She was flustered, eager and ready for the climax, and Pisces47 wanted to know her dreams?

No man had ever asked her a question like that. None had ever cared, but then again, she'd never been so selective about a partner in the past.

Even if this was just a cyberpartner.

LoveSigns.com had promised something different in cybersex. They used astrology to match partners, which had brought Scorpio63 and Pisces47 together in the first place. According to their birthdates, she and her cybermate were perfect sex partners.

And based on how she felt right now, she had to give them a grateful nod.

Pisces47 was good.

Really good.

The words repeated on the screen.

"What are your dreams, Scorpio?"

She lifted a hand to the keyboard. "I want," she typed, then clicked Send, unsure how to finish the sentence.

"Scorpio, there isn't much time. I'm aching for release. I'm going, honey. I need it now. Tell me your dreams, baby. I want to know your dreams."

Oh, jeez.

"I want love," she typed and sent.

"Then love is what I'll give you, sweetheart. A fantasy love that only we can share.

"I whisper the words in your ear as we near the edge. I'm hard, Scorpio, so hard. I'm trying to hold on, trying to last longer, but you're so warm and tight. I can't look at your beauty without losing control. I have to close my eyes, but your flowery scent is driving me closer. Come with me. Are you ready?"

"Yes," she typed.

"Your body clamps hard around me, fisting my shaft in another searing climax. You begin to cry out, but we have to be quiet. I close my mouth over yours and drink in your cries as I lose myself inside you."

And with that, she lost control. Her legs stiffened, her back coiled and a soft cry escaped her throat. The climax ripped through her, constricting every muscle from her jaw to her toes, pulsing between her legs, until the soft wave crashed over in soothing warmth.

"You collapse in my arms. Your skin is damp and those heavenly breasts are pressed against my chest. I reach down and take a bite through your shirt. Your dark, silky hair hangs down against my desk. I'm holding you in my arms, admiring the sleepy, sated smile on your face. You're so beautiful, Scorpio. I press my lips between the folds of your blouse and taste the sweet skin between your breasts. I can feel your heart beating wildly against my lips, then it slows as we rest in each other's arms."

Oh, yeah.

There was a long pause. Trisha's limp hands could barely make contact with the keyboard, and she wondered if Pisces47 felt the same way. She waited, allowing her heartbeat to slow when a message finally popped up on the screen.

"How do you feel, Scorpio?"

Her weakened fingers could only type, "Good."

"Me, too."

There was another long pause as Trisha tried to recover. She needed to return something, anything other than a few shaky pleas.

"I…" she typed, letting him know she'd be answering in a moment.

"No, Scorpio. Tonight's for you. Crawl into bed. Curl up and think of me. Think of your dreams as you rest in peaceful sleep."

She stared at the screen, the session still echoing through her mind.

"I will," she typed.

"Good night, Scorpio. And remember, honey, whenever you need me I'm just a click away."

Unable to move, she studied the words while the message popped up saying Pisces47 had logged off. She glanced around her bedroom suddenly realizing she had no idea what time it was. It had been light when they began tonight's chat, but the sun had gone down somewhere during the first climax and now the room was dark, lit only by the white screen of the chat room.

She shook herself and pressed the keys to download the chat. She'd saved all of Pisces47's chats. They were too good to toss into cyberspace, so she held them as memories of the man on the other end of the line.

Whoever he was.

Trisha's brain told her he was probably either a pudgy old married man, or a sex-starved, geeky college kid. But in her fantasies, she knew exactly who he was.

Logan Moore.

Logan had been the object of her fantasies since she'd taken her job at the Moore Agency two years ago. And for two years he'd ruined her for every man that crossed her path. In Trisha's mind, no one could stand up to Logan Moore and his dark, midnight eyes. She'd often wondered what secrets he kept in those bottomless pools.

But she'd never be the one to find out. Not only was Logan her boss, but rumor had it, the man went through women like a long-haul trucker went through diesel fuel. He was a consummate playboy with a preference toward wealthy supermodels and aspiring actresses. At least, that was the general consensus around the office, and if true, Trisha Bain was clearly out of the running.

For more than a year she'd tried to ignore her infatuation with Logan. She'd continued dating, hoping somewhere along the line Mr. Right would come along and help her forget the tall, chiseled man who filled her dreams. But she'd quickly discovered the effort was pointless. No man would be a worthy substitute for Logan Moore.

At least, not in the flesh.

That was when she happened upon LoveSigns.com and found the perfect solution. She could meet the ideal partner and carry out her sexual fantasies online, with no physical contact to remind her that the man feeding them to her was someone other than Logan Moore. She could put one man's words with another man's image and come up with the ideal mate.

For the time being.

Of course, she knew some day she'd have to move

on and doing so would probably mean quitting her job. She couldn't spend the rest of her life clinging to something that didn't really exist. And she had no intention of doing so.

Her fantasies about Logan and her account with LoveSigns.com would only take her through the next few months, when she completed the ad campaign that would be the jewel on her résumé to help her land a high-paying job somewhere else.

Just a few months of fantasies, and Trisha Bain would forget about Logan Moore and move on with her life.

At least, that was the plan.

"READY FOR THE big meeting?"

Trisha glanced up from her desk to see her friend, Adrienne, peeking through the doorway of her office.

"Not really," she replied. The pen she held jittered in her shaky hand. Not wanting to reveal her nerves, she dropped it on the desk and folded her hands in her lap. "Devon just called. His flight's delayed and he won't be back in time. It'll just be me and Logan."

The perky smile on Adrienne's face sobered as she took a step into the room. "So? This is your campaign, what do you need Devon for?"

Devon made a threesome. Without him, she'd be left alone with Logan, in his office, causing the line between reality and her fantasies to become dangerously thin.

She squeezed her hands together, digging her fingers into the backs of her knuckles. "I just…" she started, not sure how to explain, and based on Adrienne's knowing expression, she wasn't going to have to.

Adrienne reached back and closed the door. "This is about Cyber Man."

Trisha still didn't understand the complete lapse of judgment that had caused her to confess her twice-weekly chats to Adrienne. Okay, so Adrienne had been her best friend since their days at U.C. Berkeley. If she were to confess to anyone, it would be her. But given the fact that Adrienne had been against the idea from the start, she wasn't appreciating that I-told-you-so look on her face right now.

Trisha wanted sympathy, not a lecture.

She chose not to respond. Instead, she just frowned and moved her now aching hands from her lap and tucked them under her thighs.

Adrienne took a chair in front of the desk. She was making herself comfortable. She was apparently staying.

Lecture time.

"I told you that was a bad idea."

So was telling Adrienne about Cyber Man.

Adrienne stared at her for what seemed like an excruciatingly long moment, then finally smiled. "Why don't you just ask Logan out?"

What was better, the lecture or complete stupidity?

She scowled, letting Adrienne know she'd just crossed over to the latter.

"Gee, let's see," Trisha said, hoping to drag out the sarcasm in her tone. "I'm only five-foot-six, which makes me three inches too short for Logan Moore."

Trisha's height brought her eye level to his iron-pumped chest, but the six-foot-three Logan preferred women he didn't have to bend for.

"My breasts are real," she continued. "I've never been on a runway, I've never auditioned for *Baywatch* and I'm not a peroxide blonde." She released her hands from under her lap and folded them across her chest. "How many strikes is that against me?"

Adrienne scoffed. "Oh, you think you know everything. The guy dated a few bimbos after his divorce and you think you've nailed his love life. Trust me. Logan prefers women with brains."

"Sure. That Carmella Beal had quite the pair of brains. What was that she said at the awards banquet?" Trisha fluttered her eyelashes and took on a breathy tone. "'I just love the beach. It's so close to the ocean.'" Through Adrienne's giggles, she added, "Someone should embroider that one on a pillow."

"Okay, so Carmella was pretty dim, but if you've noticed, we haven't seen her since."

Trisha snorted. "She's no doubt teaching a class in physics at MIT."

"Oh, now you're just being mean."

"I am not. Believe me. Any woman who can stand erect with three-inch stilettos and double-D breasts deserves a degree in engineering."

"Logan was mortified."

"He should have been. She made him look like a complete ass." She huffed and shook her head. "He's so much better than that."

"Of course he is. We all know that was just a phase he went through after the divorce."

"Have you ever seen him with anyone normal?"

"No one has seen him with anyone at all in the last six months. I think he's given up on women."

"Well, there you have it. He gathered his jacks and went home." She thought for a moment and sighed. "No, I'm not going to risk my reputation by chasing after the boss. Sure, maybe if I thought he was interested, but Ade, the man's never so much as winked. I can't jeopardize our relationship by making a pass that's not wanted. It's not worth it."

She picked up her pen and resumed jotting down notes for the meeting. Despite Adrienne's silly notions about her and Logan, the woman had managed to calm her nerves for the moment.

"Bill thinks you two are perfect for each other."

A stab of fear stopped Trisha's heart. "You promised me you wouldn't breathe a word of this to Bill."

Adrienne had been dating Bill Jeffries, Logan's Vice President of Products and best friend, for nearly four months. Though Trisha had early reservations about the office romance, she had to admit, the two were cute as kittens together. They both had sandy-blond hair, dark eyes and matching sets of dimples that made them look as if they were born to be together. And the fact that they were still giddy lovers after four months left Trisha feeling as though they might be the real deal.

But no matter how well Adrienne's office romance was going, Trisha didn't share that same freedom when it came to Logan. Adrienne didn't report to Bill, which made them simply coworkers. Trisha, on the other hand, had her eyes set on her boss and though there wasn't a policy against office romance, dating a direct superior definitely treaded on shaky ground.

Adrienne breathed a sigh of frustration and sank back in her seat. "I've told you a dozen times, Logan and Cyber Man are between you and me."

"I mean it, Ade. A word of this gets to Logan and I'm sending an e-mail to everyone in the office telling them your real name."

Though Adrienne hadn't shed her Birkenstocks and ankle-length skirts, there were two things about her hippie, Free Age upbringing she didn't want spread around the office. One was her parents' radical political views, which included their notion that the Moore Agency was in the business of brainwashing the public to further corporate greed.

The second was her real name, Hummingbird Eucalyptus, after her mother's second-favorite bird and tree. Her older sister, Robin Willow, had been given the first choice, leaving Adrienne with a name she'd quickly found ridiculous once she'd graduated from her co-op schools and entered the real world.

Trisha rarely threatened Adrienne with their secrets, but desperate times called for desperate measures.

"I swear, Bill came up with the idea on his own."

Trisha's pulse resumed ever so slightly. "What did you tell him?"

"I told him I agree, but that it's up to you and Logan. I've done the matchmaker thing before and I swore I'd never do it again." She crossed a hand over her chest. "Honest to God."

Trisha studied her friend, looking for a twitch, a blink or a flinch that would tell her Adrienne was lying.

Nothing.

Her breathing resumed. "Thank you."

"Listen, if you aren't going to go for Logan, you need to move on with your love life. You can have practically any man you want. Why you're talking dirty on the Internet with this stranger is beyond me. You have to know he's a pimply teenaged kid."

Trisha smirked. "Or a toothless rodeo clown."

"Don't you know you're better than that?" Adrienne sighed. "Come on, sweetie, you deserve a real man. I don't know why you dumped Hal. That guy was hot."

"Ha! Harley Hal? Leather chaps aren't my style."

"Trish, the guy was hot and he adored you."

"He wanted me to get a tattoo." Trisha shook her head. "I'll never be anyone's motorcycle mamma."

"What about Phil? What was wrong with him?"

Trisha's expression went blank as she stared at Adrienne for an extended beat. "He's never had a job."

"He's in med school."

"He's a thirty-four-year-old professional student. He already has a law degree but does he try for the bar? No. He decides to go into medicine. I swear. He'll never amount to anything. He just stays in school so his parents will keep supporting him."

"His parents are filthy rich, which means he's filthy rich. What does it matter? You certainly wouldn't end up in poverty."

"I have no respect for a man who doesn't attempt to make his own way through life."

Adrienne sat back in her seat and let out a long huff. "Well, you've got to do something. Using a pimply kid to fantasize about Logan isn't getting you anywhere. You're just going to give yourself a nervous break-down." She gave Trisha the once-over. "Look at you, you're a mess," she added, pulling the pad of notes from the desk and pointing to the last few entries. "You've written the same sentence three times. Are you planning to stutter?"

"I'm just a little distracted."

"Because of Cyber Man."

"No," Trisha declared, but the tone didn't sound at all convincing.

Adrienne tossed the notes back to Trisha. "Cyber Man is a pimply teenager. Just repeat that in your head. Wipe out whatever fantasy the guy fed you and replace it with pimply teenaged kid."

Trisha doubted that was possible. She'd so thoroughly burned last night's sex chat in her mind, surgery couldn't remove the image of Logan Moore pleasuring her at his desk. Thank God, she hadn't worn her navy-blue skirt today, but if Logan wore the crisp white shirt she'd envisioned, she was going to be in trouble.

Hopefully, they would conduct the meeting at his conference table and she was considering bringing enough materials to require it, though it wasn't techni-cally necessary.

Adrienne's comment repeated in her mind. The wom-an was right. Her cybersex idea was beginning to inter-fere with her work and she would have to get over it fast before she soured her reputation and destroyed her career.

"I just need to get through this project and I'll be free to go," she said.

"You're seriously going to quit?"

"I don't have any other choice. I need to distance myself from Logan before I ruin my reputation and once I land Tyndale Resorts, I'll have the reference I need to get a good job at another agency."

"As good as what you'll have here?"

Adrienne knew something. Trisha could always read the woman like a book, especially this particular look that said she had inside information she was dying to share. She was casually glancing around the office as if she'd never seen it before while her finger tapped a countdown on the arm of her chair, as if to tick off the seconds before she burst with her news.

"What do you know?"

Adrienne's grin widened in that I-thought-you'd-never-ask smile. She straightened in her seat and leaned forward to whisper. "Well, rumor has it Logan's planning to promote you to vice president."

"Who says?"

"Came straight from Human Resources."

Reliable source, but she still found it hard to believe. She'd only been with the company two years. She was the newest marketing director on staff. But then again, none of her peers had landed the accounts she'd recently brought in the door.

She sat for a moment, trying to let the repercussions of the notion sink in.

She decided there were none.

"Well, he's wasting his time. I'm not staying. I

can't," she said, but even she could hear the uncertainty of her tone.

Adrienne's expression turned to shock. "Trish, we're talking VP. What other agency is going to make a twenty-eight-year-old woman a VP? You'd be crazy to walk away from an opportunity like that."

She hated when Adrienne was right.

"I'm going to have to give it some thought."

"You're going to have to dump Cyber Man and either make a move with Logan or get over him and find someone else." She glanced down at Trisha's hands, which had begun trembling again. "Look at you. You're a disaster. The cyber thing isn't working. You were handling Logan much better before you linked up with pimply kid."

Trisha breathed a sigh of agreement. "I know. But I really like him. Sometimes when we chat, it's like he knows me. It's almost creepy how much we think alike."

"Creepy being the operative word." Adrienne tilted her head and flashed a warm sympathetic smile that bordered on pity. "Trisha, this cybersex thing isn't for you. Dump pimply kid, get over Logan and take the VP job. Don't trash your career over a man. You can handle Logan. You just have to try."

"You're right. I know you're right," she replied.

Unfortunately, knowing and doing were two different things.

2

"Hey! What are you doing tomorrow night?"

Logan looked up from his notes to see Bill Jeffries strolling into his office with a bag of beer nuts in his hand.

He glanced at the date on his Rolex. "What's tomorrow, Thursday?"

"All day," Bill said, plopping down on one of the maple chairs that faced Logan's desk.

Without thinking, Logan muttered, "I've got a date."

Bill's eyes brightened. "Ha! I knew you couldn't swear off women forever." The stocky blonde tossed the bag of nuts on Logan's desk in a gesture of offering. "What's her name? Anyone I know?"

Logan wished he could answer that question. He had no idea who he'd been meeting twice a week in his dimly lit den. All he knew was that the more he chatted online with Scorpio63, the more intent he was to keep their dates.

He frowned at his own stupidity for making the absent comment. "It's not that kind of date."

Logan had no intention of sharing his cybertrysts with Bill, no matter how close a friend Bill was. After Logan's post-divorce escapades left him with a playboy reputation he'd never live down, the last thing he needed was the embarrassment of admitting that he was now having an Internet love affair with a woman he didn't know.

How a man in his position had been reduced to cybersex, he'd never know. It had started as a joke, a belated birthday present from his brother, Dane. Shattered by his divorce and frustrated with his new love life, Logan had thrown in the towel on dating altogether. He'd ultimately confessed his state to Dane, who in turn, signed him up with LoveSigns.com. Logan had been handed a password and a date with what he thought would be a virtual prostitute, one of those talk-dirty ladies that advertised on late-night television.

He hadn't intended to keep the date, but after four gin and tonics and nothing else to do, he'd decided, what the hell? He hadn't expected to log on and find a tender, intelligent woman, just as apprehensive as he'd been. Their first chat had been close to laughable, as bungling and awkward as real sex among strangers who weren't accustomed to such things. If he hadn't been sauced, he would have never made it through the hour. But something about the sexy, sensitive woman on the other end had him coming back and before he knew it, he was under her spell.

Sure, he told himself she was most likely some frustrated housewife. But for some reason, he simply didn't care. Scorpio63 had become the image of everything he wanted in a woman, and as pathetic as it seemed, he couldn't bring himself to let her go.

"What is it, a business meeting?" Bill asked.

"Something like that." He grabbed the bag of nuts and casually tossed one in his mouth. "So how's Megan doing with the Puffy Cream Doughnut ads?" he asked, hoping to quickly change the subject before Bill pressed him for details.

Bill didn't bite. "You're really done with women?"

Logan's beer nut turned to paste as the moisture left his mouth. He didn't want to talk about his love life. "Puffy Cream, Bill. How's it going?"

Bill snatched the bag from Logan, tipped a few nuts into his hand and tossed it back onto the desk. "Why don't you ask Trisha out? She's perfect for you."

Logan nearly choked. Trisha Bain was the last woman he cared to get involved with. And the fact that his body had other ideas made her all that more dangerous.

"She's a carbon copy of my ex," he explained.

Bill gave a sharp laugh. "Oh, come on. Trisha's nothing like Virginia."

No, Virginia Matthews, formerly Virginia Moore, was one of a kind, but she and Trisha both shared that spark to succeed at any cost, which made Trisha Bain a woman he'd need to keep far from his heart.

"She wants to do well, not take over your business," Bill added.

Logan didn't intend to give her the opportunity. He'd been a stupid young executive when he'd married his ex-wife, stupid enough to let his smaller head make the decisions and hand over control of half his business. Business she'd taken with her when she'd walked out the door. It had taken the Moore Agency three years to recover its position as one of the top ad agencies in San

Francisco, but it would take longer than that for him to recover his trust in women, especially women with the looks and brains of Trisha Bain.

"She is doing well," Logan said. "I've seen the briefs of her ads for Tyndale Resorts. She's nailed him. Landing Tyndale will be the feather in our cap that puts us back on top." *And sticks it in the craw of the lovely Virginia Matthews.* Oh, what he'd give to be there when Tyndale pulled the rug out from under his ex. He'd pay money to see the look on that surgically enhanced face when they told her she'd lost her account to the man she screwed over three years ago.

"You two make a great team."

He shot a glance at Bill. "In business, and that's where it ends. I've been there, remember? We both almost lost our jobs thanks to my brilliant choice in women."

And the fact that Trisha kept haunting his thoughts was proof he hadn't learned a thing.

After Virginia, he'd sworn off dating women in advertising, especially women at his firm. It was the only way to be sure he'd never threaten his company again. But after two years working with Trisha, he'd nearly broken the rule, the brain in his pants apparently having a shorter memory than the one between his ears. Trisha was everything that had attracted him to Virginia—a bundle of smarts, a clever wit, a killer smile, all rolled up in one tantalizing body.

It all came together as one bright neon "No" and no matter now much he tried to see their differences, the similarities between Trisha and Virginia were too obvious to ignore.

"You're forgetting one thing," Bill said. "I know Trisha. She's Adie's best friend. She's not another Virginia. And if you recall, I was the one who told you to watch out for Virginia in the first place, but you didn't listen."

No, he hadn't, Logan thought. He'd been too smitten by Virginia and too stupid to care. She'd wrapped him in such a fog, he'd believed every word she'd uttered between the sheets, her lies about wanting a family, how much she'd loved him, all the dreams about their future. And in the end it had all been a ploy to gain stake in his budding agency.

Virginia hadn't wanted a family or a husband. She'd only wanted her own agency and figured marrying a man who had one was easier than building one of her own.

The two were going to form a partnership, in business and in life. But the moment they'd made their mark, she'd dropped the bomb. Children weren't her future, marriage wasn't her bag and the only thing she wanted from him was a divorce and half his business.

He'd had to sink into debt to buy her out, giving her the money and status she needed to start a business of her own and then slowly snatch his accounts, one by one. He'd managed to restore his business, but the damage she'd done to his faith in his instinct was irreparable. How he'd been so colossally blind was a question for the ages, but he'd bought it all at a hefty price tag.

And it was a mistake he wouldn't repeat.

"I'm not interested," he said.

"Suit yourself, man. But one of these days, you should start listening to your old buddy here. I know what's good for you."

"So why are you asking me about tomorrow night?" Logan asked, trying once again to change the subject.

"Adie and I are going to a club to listen to some band she discovered. We were trying to get a few people to go along with us."

Logan raised an eyebrow. "What few people?"

"Nobody, just a couple friends, that's all."

The caged look on Bill's face told him those couple of friends included Trisha Bain.

"Stop trying to fix me up with Trisha," Logan insisted.

"I'm not. Trisha's not even going."

Confusion set in. If Bill's plans didn't involve match-making, then something else was up.

Logan narrowed his eyes. "What are you really doing tomorrow?"

Bill opened his mouth, but nothing came out. He stuttered a moment before finally confessing through a long exhale, "Okay, so it's some sort of…poetry reading."

Logan threw his head back and laughed.

"Oh, come on, man. Adrienne's mom is making her go. I guess it's something special and she wants the whole family to be there."

"I'm not family."

"There will be music afterward."

"What, a sitar?" Logan asked through his chuckle.

"Probably."

"I don't think so." Although the thought of watching Bill trying to order a beer in some hippie tea house was tempting.

"Aw, come on. Help me out."

Logan looked at Bill in amazement. "Are you kidding? My ears are still bleeding from that punk rock festival you dragged me to last year." He shook his head in disgust. "What was *her* name?"

"Fawn and it was alternative rock, not punk."

"It's all the same to me."

"You're just an old fart."

"And you've got bizarre taste in women," Logan added under his breath. "At least Adrienne's a move in the right direction."

"And so is Trisha. I don't know why you don't go for her. You two would make a nice conservative couple, elevator music and all."

Logan ignored the slam and shook his head. "Forget about me and Trisha. I have plans for her and none of them include sleeping with her."

Bill perked. Insider information was his favorite joy in life. The man relished being in on a secret, and sometimes Logan truly believed that Bill was a thirteen-year-old girl in a past life.

"Spill, big guy. Don't keep me in the dark."

Logan smiled and paused, dragging out the tension. He loved toying with Bill, just as Bill loved toying with him. It was a little game they'd been playing since they'd met ten years ago.

Bill held up his hands. "Well?"

"Tyndale's going to be big. He's got six resorts along the west coast, with plans to open another in the Caribbean. If we get the account, we'll need to hire more staff." He picked up the bag of nuts and studied them for a moment, extending Bill's agony for as long as possible. "I think Trisha would make a good candidate to head up a new travel segment."

"So the VP rumor is true."

Logan slammed the bag on the desk as Bill's smirk told him he'd just been duped. "Son of a bitch. I can't trust Sally with a goddamned thing." He was more annoyed by losing his match with Bill than the knowledge that his Human Resources manager had loose lips.

Bill's heavy chest rumbled as he laughed. "Sor-a-mundo, buddy boy. I already knew."

"Well, keep it to yourself, although that's probably pointless. I haven't made my decision yet, and if we don't get Tyndale, we don't have enough business to form a separate segment. I don't want Trisha disappointed if it doesn't happen."

"Don't worry about it. You'll get Tyndale and everything will work out as planned. I'm sure of it."

PIMPLY KID, pimply kid, pimply kid.

Trisha hesitated outside Logan's door for a beat as she repeated the mantra in her head, trying to lose the nerves that held on like an angry cold. She'd hoped some miracle would have brought Devon back in time to join her in Logan's office, but her last-minute check found him still sitting in O'Hare.

She was on her own.

She took one giant breath, exhaled the memory of the previous night's chat and stepped into the office.

One look at Logan behind his desk sucked the image back to her mind. Not only was he wearing the starched white shirt she'd envisioned the night before, but he'd removed his tie and unbuttoned the top two buttons, showing a faint hint of dark hair that told her his rock-like chest had the perfect blend of curls that made him masculine but not too hairy.

He'd rolled up his sleeves to the elbows and his hands were planted firmly on the arms of his chair, his fingers splayed over the ends, just as she'd seen it in her head.

She briefly made eye contact. Just enough to catch him sweep his dark eyes over her body in a manner that stopped short of lustful appreciation. He kept it professional, but sincere. Just a glance that made her wonder if he was interested, but didn't reveal enough to answer the question.

It still sent a blizzard of tingles through her chest that twirled down to the spot between her thighs.

Her hands went numb, as if she'd just been shot with a local anesthetic. She attempted to wiggle her fingers, but they remained cemented to the files she clutched to her chest.

He lifted his hand and waved to her. "Come on in."

For a brief millisecond her feet wouldn't move. She didn't want to sit at his desk. The image of sitting *on* it kept elbowing to the front of her thoughts. But she couldn't come up with a plausible reason to ask him to move to the table.

Reluctantly she stepped inside, trying to keep her eyes focused on anything other than Logan Moore and those lips that, just last night, had been planted firmly between her—

Another clench between the legs told her to calm

down and let it go. She was a professional. She hadn't made it to where she was by lusting over something as silly as a few open shirt buttons.

She picked up her pace and casually took a seat across from him. She just wouldn't look at him. They were here to discuss her ad campaign, not to gaze into each other's eyes.

Without a word of greeting, she dropped the folders onto the desk and opened the first. She pulled the now sweaty pen from her left hand and flipped open her notebook preparing to get down to business.

"So this is what we've got," she said. "I think Tyndale is going to like these ads."

"Good afternoon to you, too, Trisha."

She slowly brought her eyes from the ads to his face. His mouth was cocked in a half-smile, she could swear his gaze had just been planted on her chest, and when their eyes locked, a bolt of lightning shot through her, curling her toes.

Don't look at his eyes.

She quickly glanced to his hair and those dark, wavy curls that she'd had her fingers threaded through on a number of imaginary occasions.

Hair, bad.

She shot her eyes down to his chest.

No, not the chest.

His ear, she could focus on his ear, she thought, before remembering she'd nibbled on it last Tuesday.

As her eyes shot around his features like a pinball, she realized she was sinking without a net. She needed to pull it together. She quickly glanced at the bronze

Remington statue that stood on the credenza behind him. A team of wild horses. How fitting. She'd need a team of horses to jolt the lust from her head.

"You're always business, aren't you, Trisha?"

Her eyes met his as she mentally slapped herself in the face. It was time to act like a grown woman, like a company director who was supposedly slated for a VP position at the prestigious Moore Agency. And if she wanted that spot, she was going to have to prove to herself that she could overcome this lust for her boss and act maturely instead of being some sort of flustered teenager.

She cleared her throat, took a deep breath and began acting like a woman who belonged in the business world.

"I'm just excited about this campaign. I think we'll get the contract. We've come up with some ideas that match the tone of the resorts and the image Marc Tyndale wants to portray. You'll be impressed."

He glanced down to the files. "I'm always impressed when it comes to you."

Not helping.

"I appreciate that."

With his elbows propped on the armrests, he laced his fingers together and tilted back his chair, relaxed, casual and entirely sexy. His movement caused a light breeze of his aftershave to sweep up her nose, sending another intoxicating wave of heat through her midsection.

"I only have one problem when it comes to you, Trisha."

That iced her down and grabbed her attention.

She studied him, waiting for an explanation.

His brief grin let her know he'd noticed the look of concern on her face. "Trisha, you work too hard. There's only a couple nights a week you leave here on time."

Those would be the nights she cut out to have imaginary sex with her boss.

He pulled up his chair and leaned his arms on the desk, moving a little too close for her comfort.

"What I'm getting at is, I don't want to be responsible for ruining your personal life."

Too late.

"If you need another assistant," he continued, "please just say the word."

She exhaled the breath she'd been holding and forced herself to relax.

"I appreciate that, but Devon and I are fine."

He raised an eyebrow.

"Really," she insisted. "If I feel it's too much, I'll tell you, but for now, I'm fine."

"Uh-huh. And I assume your boyfriend would agree?"

She opened her mouth, but any attempt at words would have only resulted in a low gurgle in her throat. Logan had never made reference to her personal life before. He'd always remained strictly business, and being that he was the reason she had no boyfriend, she wasn't sure how to answer.

His smile turned to reluctance. "I'm sorry, I didn't mean to pry into your personal life."

"No, please." She couldn't let her silence make him feel like a cad. "It's just…I don't have a boyfriend, that's all."

Logan's eyes darkened. She couldn't tell if it was disbelief, or suspicion, but something inside him turned, and for the life of her, she didn't understand why.

Why would Logan care that she was unattached? And why would he react with such obvious distaste? Plenty of people in the office were single. Logan himself was single, uninvolved in a serious relationship.

What did it matter to him?

And without a doubt, it mattered.

It was written all over his face.

She opened her mouth to inquire, but he cut her off.

"There's more to life than work. You're already doing a great job, you don't need to do more and I need to know that you can delegate responsibility."

Well, there it was. The hint that Adrienne's VP rumor might actually be true.

"I'm just giving extra attention to Tyndale. I know how important this particular account is to you."

A faint smile crossed his face. "It is important, but I won't sacrifice my staff to get it. Besides, I need you rested for the sales pitch next week."

A lump formed in Trisha's throat. This was exactly the glimpse inside Logan Moore that snatched her heart and twisted it in knots. It was this caring, supportive side of Logan that he didn't often show, but when he did, it made her want to unpeel those layers of stoic professionalism to see what was truly inside.

"I appreciate that," she said. "And I promise, once these go to print, I'll take some time off."

He cleared his throat and took the folder in his

hands. "I suppose that's a reasonable deal. So let's get the ball rolling."

"SORRY I'm late."

Trisha dropped her purse on the kitchen counter of her parents' Tiburon home, pressed a kiss to her mother's cheek and took a seat at the bar next to her brother Mark.

"Devon's been out of town and I've had to handle everything," she added.

"No worries," her father said. "I'm just putting on the potatoes. We won't be eating for at least a half hour."

"How is the Tyndale campaign coming?" her mother asked.

"Good. Logan seems pleased and I think we've got a solid shot at the account."

She grabbed a wineglass from the counter and poured herself a glass of Bordeaux, ready to put the day behind her and relax in the company of her family. Despite their busy schedules, everyone still gathered twice a month for dinner with the folks. It was a ritual they'd shared since childhood.

Her parents both had hectic careers, her father, Phillip, an economics professor at U.C. Berkeley, and her mother, Monica, an executive for Sunwest Bank. But no matter how demanding their careers, her parents had always made sure the family sat down to a meal together at least once a week. The tradition had lasted through Trisha's childhood, and even though the kids had grown and moved out, they all kept returning for the weekly meal that only recently had dropped back to twice a month.

Her parents had never insisted they make it, the dinners were simply an open invitation to whoever could come. But they always did. Her older sister, Cheryl, was a stay-at-home mom of two young toddlers and these dinners were her opportunity to get off her feet and let someone else do the cooking for a change.

Trisha's younger brother, Mark, was still in college working toward a doctorate in psychology and he never turned down the chance to come home, laundry in tow.

For Trisha, the visits were her way of staying grounded, the frequent reminder of what she wanted from life. Watching her parents work together was her way of staying real, the scene before her reflecting everything she hoped to find in a marriage someday. Her mother and father loved cooking together and had perfected the task to an art. They bustled around the kitchen like two lovers in a dance and it was a symbol of how they shared their lives. Juggling careers and three children wasn't an easy task, but Phillip and Monica Bain had always made it look easy, their deep respect for each other and unyielding camaraderie working together to make a success of their lives and their family.

They had become the litmus test Trisha used when evaluating a current lover. If a man didn't treat her like her father treated her mother, he wasn't long in the arms of Trisha Bain. Though she admitted her parents were a hard act to follow, she always believed she could find that special someone who could work with her through life like her parents worked together.

Like she and Logan did at the office.

She blinked away the errant thought, insisting on keeping that subject on the shelf while she enjoyed dinner with her family.

"So, you're just in time to help me," Mark said as Cheryl took a seat at the bar.

"Help with what?" she asked.

"Valentine's Day is coming up and I need some ideas on what to get Grace."

"Getting serious about Grace, are we?" Monica asked as she snapped peas into a large glass bowl.

"Maybe. I'm not ready for the altar, but I think a woman who can handle me through finals deserves something nice."

Cheryl chuckled. "She deserves sainthood."

"Okay, so short of that, what should I get her?"

"That's easy. Diamonds and gold."

"I said I'm not ready for the altar."

"I was thinking necklace, idiot."

Mark mulled over the suggestion. "What do you think, Mom?"

"A necklace would be nice, or maybe a bracelet."

He turned to Trisha. "Anyone give you jewelry for Valentine's Day?"

Trisha tried to remember getting *anything* on Valentine's Day, but none of her relationships seemed to make it to that level. Somehow, before things got serious, she'd always found some sort of deal breaker in a man that nixed their future together—a thought that left her wondering about the choices she'd made in the past.

She considered the question. "No jewelry, but Hal had taken me for a motorcycle ride up the coast. That was kind of sweet. He'd told me to bring my camera and we'd stop and shoot some landscapes along the way."

Trisha had a passion for nature photography, and she'd remembered thinking how sweet it was that Hal had considered her hobby when planning their day.

"Although," she recalled, "it didn't turn out the way I'd hoped."

"God, I remember that." Cheryl chuckled. "You ended up in some dingy bar, didn't you?"

"The place was a dive. I spent the whole time worrying my camera would get stolen."

"What were you doing with that guy?" Cheryl asked. "He was so not you."

Trisha took a sip of her wine. "I fell for his body and forgot there was a personality inside."

"He was hot," Cheryl agreed. "Tell me, is it true what they say about the size of a man's hands? That guy had some big hands."

"I'm not hearing this," their father proclaimed.

Cheryl rolled her eyes. "Come on, Dad, we're grown women. How do you think you ended up with two grandchildren?"

Phillip gasped and jokingly turned to his wife. "You told me that was divine intervention!"

"It was, honey." Monica winked. "Cheryl's just pulling your leg."

"Can we get back to gift ideas?" Mark asked, that baby-brother whine still evident in his voice at the age of twenty-five.

"I told you," Cheryl said. "Women are easy. Buy her a necklace. Grace will love it. Men are the hard ones to buy for. I never know what to get Steve." She looked at their father. "Dad, what was the best Valentine's present Mom ever gave you?"

"That's easy. I got a lovely handmade card telling me we were going to have a baby. And eight months later, you were born."

"Seven," Monica said. "Remember? All my babies were early."

Phillip chuckled. "You almost delivered Trisha in the middle of a business meeting. I remember the nurses saying you were the best-dressed screaming woman they'd ever seen."

Monica groaned. "That was awful. My water broke right in the middle of a roomful of bankers."

"If you ask me," Mark chimed in, "I think Trisha just wanted to join the meeting."

"I'm so sure," Trisha scoffed.

"Get real. You were born in a business suit and your career is your red-hot lover. You've always been that way."

Had she? Admittedly, she'd always aspired to be like her mother, showing up at dance recitals in those sharp business suits and her hair twisted in a perfect French roll. Trisha had been so proud to show her off, and at a very young age, had aspired to be just like her.

But was that the path she was on? Looking around the room, she realized she was the only one in the family who hadn't found a serious relationship. Even her little brother had stumbled across that someone special, while Trisha had put her career before every-thing.

Is that what she really wanted?

Watching her parents together, the answer was a re-sounding no. Their careers were only a part of their lives, not the sum of it, and Trisha wondered if she'd been too focused on first things first. Admittedly, a woman didn't make vice president at her age without making her job a priority. But that wasn't what she'd wanted and the whole issue had her rethinking her priorities.

Her mother hadn't become an executive until all the children were grown. For most of their lives, she'd just been a branch manager, a job that required little travel and half the responsibility she shouldered now. And as if to make it worse, Trisha had chosen advertising, a career with sharp deadlines and plenty of extra hours. Maybe the VP prospect wasn't the greatest idea. Not only would it up the ante on the pressures at work, but the Tyndale account would have her on the road for weeks on end.

No wonder Logan had been so concerned about her home life. Maybe he'd seen what she hadn't—that she'd set aside everything for a fast path to the top, and the thought that it concerned him left an ache in her heart. It was just another reason she needed a man like him, someone who could cut through the fog and re-mind her that life was about more than work and business.

And if she wanted that life, maybe she would need to set the VP job aside and look for work at another agency. Staying focused on what she wanted was hard enough without pining over a man she couldn't have. Between her tendency to put her career first and this unending lust for her boss, she was blending a cocktail of misery that she might later regret.

"Mark, don't be so hard on your sister," their mother said.

"No, Mom," Trisha replied. "I think that's exactly what I needed to hear."

3

Daily Love Horoscope for Pisces

Your usual intuitive nature is more analytical than normal today making this an ideal time to assess your romantic prospects. Consider all your options, take the ones that work for you and don't be afraid to toss the ones that don't.

"TAKE ME somewhere tropical."

The words on the screen left Logan intrigued. Scorpio63 always preferred office fantasies, which was fine by him. When it came to Scorpio, he'd follow her anywhere she wanted to go. But the idea of a clear blue ocean, sparkling white sand and a warm salty breeze sounded darn good, too, just proving that Scorpio63 was an endless well of surprises.

"Mmm, I'm picturing you topless in a sapphire-blue thong," he typed, and clicked Send.

"I've just come from the beach. My hair is wet. Droplets of water trickle down my back. As I step through the hotel suite, I toss away my bikini top. It was wet and the water cools on my skin as I cross the air-conditioned room. My breasts are tight and firm, dotted with goose bumps and the cold air hardens my nipples.

"It's chilly in the room. I want to warm up, so I step onto the terrace and lean against the railing of the balcony, letting the warm breeze melt away the chill."

This was good, he thought as a layer of warmth spread throughout his body.

"You didn't see me enter the room," he typed. "You thought I was still in town on business, but the meeting ended early. I've just come from a swim in the pool and I'm naked except for the towel draped around my waist."

"I can sense you behind me, standing in the doorway to the balcony. A soft wind blows, I can smell the chlorine in your hair. It smells sharp, but fresh."

"The sight of your ass makes me hard. It's bare except for the band of blue fabric separating those silky cheeks. Water trickles down your back and trails into the crease. I want to be there, too."

And, oh, did he ever. He closed his eyes and played the scene over in his mind, causing a wave of heat to spill through his veins and harden his loin. He raised his hands to the keyboard about to add more when Scorpio's words rolled onto the screen.

"I'm leaning against the railing. The warm air feels good against my skin, but the feel of your hands gently covering my breasts feels better. Your lips begin to suckle the nape of my neck and I shiver from your touch."

The image raised a tent in his sweats as he sank back into his leather den chair and let Scorpio take control.

"Your fingers pinch my nipples and the sensation

snatches my breath. I hear your towel whoosh to the floor as it pools around our feet. While your hands continue to tease me, I feel your hard shaft against my back. It's so big, so ready. I step my feet apart, so you can stroke your length between my thighs."

Man, why hadn't they left the office before?

As the pressure stiffened his cock, he joined in. "I release my hands from your breasts and smooth them down your waist until my thumbs tug against your thong. I latch on and pull the fabric down your legs. You kick it off your feet, and while I'm bent, I see your fleshy ass in my face and I can't help but take a bite. I bring a finger to your sex and nearly come when I feel the slick heat, pulsing, ready for me."

"I want you, Pisces. I want you to fill me from behind while I feel the breeze against my face. The air is getting hot and beads of sweat are glistening on my skin. My breath is heavy. I can feel the heat from your lungs as you clasp your mouth to my shoulder and nibble on my skin. I feel pain and pleasure all at the same time and it sears heat between my thighs."

"Scorpio, you're making me hard. My cock is so stiff and I ache to get inside you. I'm stroking it in the cleavage of your ass, but it's not enough. I need that slick heat of your core."

Logan grew harder, ready to put some action into this fantasy they'd started, but Scorpio took the reins.

"I grasp the railing. Your hands clasp my waist. You're tall. You have to bend to place your cock between my thighs. My back is arched, my ass is pressing against your waist, waiting for you to take me.

"Are you ready, Pisces?"

He stared at the words on the screen, not quite believing what he was seeing. Scorpio had never been this bold before and he quickly began to wonder what she had in store for him.

He raised a hand to the keyboard and typed, "Yes."

"You guide your cock to my entrance, and in one quick motion, you thrust inside, lifting my hips as you stand erect, pulling my feet from the ground."

Damn. The blood rushed to his cock, bringing a searing ache between his legs. His mouth went arid, the room grew hot and his heart raced as he waited to see what she'd do next.

"My legs dangle at your sides and you wrap your hands around my thighs, using your fingers to tease between my folds. I'm at your mercy, Pisces. I wiggle against you, but in this position, I have nowhere to go. I've surrendered control and all I can do is watch the waves of the ocean and feel the pleasure you bring."

Logan swallowed the lump in his throat. He'd never seen Scorpio so hot, so commanding, and her words sent sparks through his chest, speeding his pulse. Once again, he raised a hand to the keyboard, ready to take over the fantasy, and once again, Scorpio yanked it back.

"You're holding me with your stiff length, caressing your fingers between my thighs. In this position, I'm tight. You can't stroke inside me. You can only go deeper, using the weight of my body to sink farther inside."

A sharp bolt swelled his already throbbing cock.

They hadn't done anything like this before and he quickly decided he liked it.

"I'm gasping, fighting for breath, Pisces. You're deep inside me, but I want more. I want you to thrust harder, faster."

"You cup your hands around my sex and heave into me. I cry out and my cries are a mix of ecstasy and awe. I clamp tight around you, the muscles between my legs are the only muscles I control and I beg you to use that spot to make me come."

Logan's breath grew short, his hardness ached beyond anything he'd ever known, and with Scorpio at the helm, he conceded to reach into his sweats and pleasure himself into release.

"Your fingers brush against my clit while you thrust against me from behind. You can feel me growing in your hand, just like your cock is growing inside me."

Oh, heaven help me. He grabbed a towel and quickened the stroke of his hand.

"Sweat drips off your forehead and trickles down my back. My breathing has turned to heavy pants, each exhale mixed with a pleading cry. I'm close to the edge, Pisces. I'm ready, and this time, the orgasm is going to tear us apart."

That was an understatement.

"You're clasping your fingers over me, taking me hard and fast. My legs sway at your sides as you thrust against me. My hands clamp tightly to the railing, my cries are growing louder and with one final sweep, I gulp in air and clamp tight around your shaft. My body stiffens, my knees bend and my feet curl around your legs. The orgasm is ripping through me, fisting around you so tightly, you can't pull back. I'm pulsing against your finger and you hear me exhale your name in a deep cry that echoes down the deserted beach below us."

Logan stared at the screen as he neared the edge of climax, slowing his stroke to prolong the sensation. Never before had Scorpio turned him this hard, this fast, and he wondered what had happened to release this sexy siren.

"I buckle against you. I want you to pull your fingers from between my folds. The sensation is too severe. But with each brush of your finger, I clamp you, massaging your cock, sucking it in to the point where you're about to explode.

"You cup your hand over me and squeeze until I cry out again, and with one more thrust, you burst, filling me, relieving us both."

Logan closed his eyes as a heavy grunt escaped his chest with the orgasm ripping through him, curving his back, sucking the wind from his lungs. Through the rushing release, he could barely read the words on the screen.

"You're bucking against me. You've lost control and now my knees are scraping against the hard wood of the railing. You pull your fingers from between my legs and clamp your hands to my hips, pulling me farther from the ground, pushing my body against the rail as you let go inside me."

His heart beating wildly, he quickened his stroke and pumped the last of his climax—a climax that seemed to never end—until finally, his arms fell limp at his sides.

"My chin falls to my chest and my hair splays over the railing. You press your lips to my back and slip from my core, pull me into your arms and carry me to the bed. My sex still throbs. You stretch your body out next to mine and we rest on the bed as the warm ocean breeze flutters against the sheer curtains and dances across the room."

Logan had no reply. He didn't know what to do. This was the most intense session he'd ever had with Scorpio. He'd never seen her so filled with fire and his heart ached more than ever to know who she really was.

Oh, if only Scorpio was a woman who he could touch and explore in the flesh instead of through the cold keys of his computer. But a side of him didn't want to lose the fantasy woman. For the last few months, Scorpio63 had been the one woman he could truly count on, truly trust, and despite his desire to taste her for real, he didn't want to ruin what they'd created.

He raised a limp hand to the keyboard.

"Scorpio," he typed.

"Yes, Pisces?"

"You're amazing."

There was a short pause before the words appeared on the screen. "Tonight is for you, Pisces. It's our special tropical retreat. A secret place where just the two of us can go."

"I like that, Scorpio."

"Good night, Pisces."

He raised his fingers to the keyboard, wanting to type the words that would keep her with him for a while longer. Often, they'd shared their thoughts and feelings before or after sex, and tonight, he wanted more. But Scorpio was cutting out, possibly because she had to, so he reluctantly let her go.

"Good night, sweetheart," he typed. "And remember, whenever you need me, I'm just a click away."

He pushed back from his desk and stepped through his flat on the waters of San Francisco's marina to soak in the early evening scenery. The late January skies were unusually clear tonight, giving him a spectacular view of the bay that stretched past Alcatraz to the shores of Marin beyond. A lone jogger huffed along the Marina Green, his breath coming out as fog in the chilly night air. Beyond him, a vast cargo ship inched along the water on its way to the Oakland Harbor.

This was the view he paid handsomely for and he wished he were enjoying it with Scorpio in his arms instead of standing here alone.

He'd almost asked her for her name tonight, and if she'd given him time, he might have. But his better judgment had kept him silent. LoveSigns.com wasn't a matchmaking site. The advertising was fully directed at anonymity, knowing the less couples knew about each other, the more freedom they'd have to express their sexual fantasies. And that's what Love-Signs.com was all about. Fantasy. There were plenty of dating services for people looking for a mate. This site was marketed as purely entertainment, a place for people to go when they wanted to escape reality and relish in a thrill.

Though Logan hadn't been looking for fantasies,

he knew other subscribers were and given that Scorpio had never suggested sharing information, he was almost certain she wasn't looking for anything more.

Moving from the large bay window, he grabbed his cell phone and turned it on to check messages, finding only one. His brother, Dane, had called twenty minutes earlier, and Logan dialed the code to hear the message.

"Hey, where are you? I'm dying here! Sonja's been gone three days and I'm crawling out of my skin. You said you'd be home tonight. Call me. I'm bored. I need to get out of this house and I can't find a solitary soul to hang out with. You're my last resort."

His last resort?

Logan dialed the number and waited for Dane to answer.

"Hello?"

"Nice to know I'm so high on your list of priorities," he said flatly.

"Huh?"

Logan grinned. "Never mind. What do you want to do?"

"There's open gym at the club tonight. Shoot some hoops? Loser buys beers."

He looked at his watch. It was still early, and sitting here thinking about his love life didn't sound like a plan. Between Scorpio and Trisha, he'd managed to work himself into a mood and beating his brother on the basketball court usually did wonders to lift his spirits.

"You're on. I'll meet you there in fifteen minutes?"

"Make it ten."

"YOUR GAME WAS OFF tonight," Dane said, sipping a beer at O'Malley's, an Irish pub on Geary that was close to the gym Logan and Dane belonged to. "I actually won."

"I'm feeling generous, figured I'd buy the beer this evening. Besides, you sounded pretty pathetic on the phone. I decided you didn't need any more humiliation." He slugged back a gulp of his pale ale and asked, "So what's up? You said Sonja's out of town?"

"She's in Italy doing a shoot. And before that, she'd just spent a week down south." Dane shook his head. "This schedule of hers is killing me. I may need to call in reinforcements or find someone who doesn't travel so damn much." He looked at his brother with all seriousness. "Don't ever date a fashion model."

Logan didn't intend to, discovering after his divorce that the women in Dane's address book definitely weren't his type.

He glanced at his brother and asked, "Have you ever thought about finding a nice local girl and settling down?"

"No."

Dane made the comment without the slightest flinch or hesitation, and Logan knew he'd asked a stupid question. His little brother was a consummate playboy with a black book full of beautiful women who preferred their men fast and noncommittal. Logan couldn't understand the lifestyle. When it came to Dane's type, the sex might be fun for a minute, but the moment you wanted to talk about something deeper than the weather, you got nothing but air.

To Logan, women were a package that included a

body and a brain, and he'd never been able to appreciate the former if it wasn't accompanied by the latter.

The thought brought him back to Trisha. Why the hell couldn't she have been his real estate agent or dry cleaner instead of his employee? The hassle—he didn't need, he'd just gotten past his divorce, restored his business and his personal life from the shambles they had become. He'd lived a life of celibacy for some time and that was quickly running cold. He was ready to seek out someone who might be able to offer a second chance.

And the first woman to tempt him had to be the ultimate in forbidden fruit.

How was that for fate?

"I'm fine," Dane insisted. "You're the one who needs help with the opposite sex." He leaned back and propped his feet on an empty chair, giving him a better view of the bar and the dozen or so men and women sharing drinks over darts and pool. Dane was perpetually on the prowl.

"So have you still opted out of the dating game, or are you finally coming to your senses?" he added.

"There's a couple women who've interested me."

Unfortunately, one was off limits and the other was a fantasy, probably living in a trailer in Cheyenne, Wyoming.

"Yeah? Tell me about them."

He'd rather not. Discussing Scorpio63 was out of the question. He hadn't even admitted to Dane that he'd logged on to the site. Telling him he'd fallen for his virtual sex partner was out of the question.

Discussing Trisha was equally unappealing, although Dane would definitely give him a fresh, if not sordid, perspective where that was concerned. Given the state he was in, he could use the advice, no matter how one-sided it would probably be.

He took a swig of his beer and decided, what the hell?

"There's a woman at the agency," Logan started. "Smart, funny, killer body. She's top in her game."

"What is she, a secretary?"

"Marketing director." He popped a pretzel in his mouth and added, "I'm thinking of promoting her to VP."

Dane threw his head back and spoke to the ceiling. "What are you, a masochist or just brain dead?"

"I know what you're thinking."

"Then what the hell are you doing? Logan, you're just getting the business back on track. Have you got some kind of aversion toward success?"

"Bill doesn't think she's another Virginia."

Dane stared at him blankly. "Bill's an idiot."

Dane calling Bill an idiot was like Moe Howard calling Larry Fine a stooge. Neither of them were the brightest bulbs when it came to women, which was why Logan fit right in. In this kingdom of idiots, he'd be the court jesters since Bill and Dane were happy with their love lives and hadn't managed to destroy their careers, which gave them one leg up on him.

Deciding to play devil's advocate, he went on. "Bill could be right."

"Okay," Dane said, apparently willing to play. "Let me ask a few questions."

"Shoot."

"How long has she worked there?"

"Two years."

"And you're already thinking VP?"

"She deserves it. Advertising's in her blood. She's a natural, someone I intend to keep."

"So she's another woman on a fast track to the top."

"Not necessarily. She hasn't expressed displeasure with her position. If you recall, Virginia had been the one pushing for promotions. This woman hasn't uttered a word."

"But you're going to do it anyway."

"If she lands this account, we'll need a VP. She's good. I've got no reason to pass her up for someone else."

"And I take it if you're interested that means she's available."

"Yes," Logan said, that chilling feeling returning to his gut.

He'd been shocked when she'd told him she didn't have a boyfriend. A woman like Trisha should have been snatched up years ago; he couldn't help recall that same surprise when he'd met Virginia. Back then, he'd chalked it up to his good luck. This time, it gave him that eerie feeling history was repeating itself.

"But that doesn't have to mean anything," he added, as much for himself as for Dane. "Lots of bright, attractive women are available."

"And they all happen to work for you."

"I think I'm just being paranoid."

"I think you're just being a fool. What happened to swearing off women in advertising? Logan, you can have any woman you want in this city. Why someone who works for you?"

Because that's where he spent all his time. Rebuilding a company hadn't left him with much of a social life, and besides, he happened to like women who shared that common bond.

"Dating Virginia wasn't my downfall. Marrying her and making her a full partner was."

"And you think you've got what it takes to be a life-long bachelor? Come on, Logan. You were always the marrying type."

Not anymore. He'd been burned once, he wouldn't be burned again. Any woman in his future would have to accept marriage only if and when he chose it. Virginia had pushed for that contract. She'd delivered an ultimatum—marriage or nothing—and rather than lose her, he'd uttered "I do" and walked straight into disaster.

That was one threshold he wouldn't cross until *he* felt ready and if an ultimatum came sooner than that the next woman would get a very different answer.

"Maybe I am, but I won't be pushed there, and the right woman will accept that."

"You really believe that?"

He gulped the last of his beer. "That's the only thing I'm sure of."

Trisha looked over the final mock-ups of their presentation for Tyndale's Cape Horn resort, stacked the pages in her folder and walked down to Logan's office, hoping he would be there. She needed his final approval today to have the materials ready for the meeting with the Tyndale folks.

Since his personal assistant wasn't at her desk, she peeked around the open door to find him talking on the phone. Logan glanced up and as usual waved a hand for her to enter, raising a finger to indicate he'd be just a moment.

She stepped into the room and waited, allowing her eyes to admire the strong hollows of his cheeks that turned to creases when he smiled.

He chuckled, his laugh spinning sparks in her chest. He had the sexiest laugh she'd ever heard, low and easy, the kind that she could easily envision hearing in the dark, between the sheets.

She blinked away the thought. She'd come too far these last few days in her effort to get over Logan. Moving her chats with Pisces out of the office had been a start. Their Caribbean fantasy had done wonders to calm her nerves and her nine-to-five life. She'd eased up around Logan and wasn't about to start losing it now.

She turned her gaze to the window, allowing her mind to focus on the bright sunny afternoon and the soft sparkle of light that flickered off the windows of an adjacent building. She stepped to the window. Looking down at the wharf, she noted the bay was also calm today. The sky was a bright shade of blue and she found something relaxing in the bustle of the street below.

Her mind was at ease as she shifted her thoughts from the man behind the desk to the task at hand. She was truly pulling it together and the notion left her pleased.

Until a comment from Logan swept it all away.

"You've got it," he said, adding, "Well, whenever you need me, I'm just a click away."

The folder dropped from her hand, scattering papers onto the floor, but Trisha barely noticed. Her mouth hung open and her eyes fixed on Logan as he hung up the phone, his parting statement echoing in her ears.

Whenever you need me, I'm just a click away.

How many people said that? Was it common? She'd never heard it from anyone other than Pisces47—*and now Logan Moore*. The repercussions began to spin in her head with the force of a tornado. She couldn't think, couldn't move. All she could do was stare blankly while she tried desperately to make her lungs expand and take in air.

"Trisha," she heard him say, but she couldn't respond, her mind reeling.

He rose from his desk, his face riddled with concern. "Are you okay?"

She glanced down to see her ad campaign splayed at her feet.

He rushed from his desk and reached out to touch her, and the sight of his hand nearing her shoulder made her jump. She tried to hide it by squatting to the floor, her shaking fingers attempting to gather the ads.

"You look like you've seen a ghost."

A ghost. Right now, she'd welcome a ghost, or a serial killer or a nine-point-nine earthquake—anything that would distract her from the conclusions filling her brain and sickening her stomach.

"I just…" she ventured. "I just remembered I was supposed to make a phone call."

She quickly gathered the ads and stashed them in the folder. "The place is going to close. It's important."

She jumped to her feet and shoved the folder into his hands. "Can I leave these with you?" she said as she rushed to the door, trying to keep her pace from a full-throttled run.

"Sure," he said, but the look on his face told her he wasn't buying her story.

"I'll…" She didn't know what to say. She didn't want to see Logan Moore right now. Not until she collected her thoughts and stopped the fear that stabbed her heart.

"I may have to leave early. I'll have Devon stop in before he goes home."

She heard him utter faint agreement as she bolted from the office.

4

TRISHA HEADED STRAIGHT to the ladies' room. It was the only place she could go where she knew he couldn't follow. And she feared he might.

She knew she must have turned white as a sheet, and Logan wasn't stupid. She doubted that he believed her lie but right now the only thing that mattered was getting away from him and figuring out what to do.

She held up both hands and pushed open the door, feeling only a slight breath of relief when the door closed behind her.

Could Logan really be Pisces47?

She prayed it wasn't true.

Martha Andrews, one of her coworkers, emerged from a stall, her eyes narrowing when she caught sight of Trisha at the sink.

"Are you okay?"

"Martha, please do me a favor. Would you go get Adrienne, tell her to come in here? It's urgent."

Martha's eyes scanned over her. "Sure," she said, reluctance tingeing her tone. "Are you okay?" she repeated.

"Yes. I just…need to see Adrienne."

Martha quickly rinsed her hands, pulled a towel from the dispenser and dried them on her way out. "I'll get her right now."

"Thank you."

She tried to calm her nerves as she waited. Adrienne would tell her she was crazy, that this was just coincidence and all would be fine.

"Trisha?"

Adrienne's voice brought welcome relief and she was suddenly thankful she'd confessed Cyber Man to her friend. Right now, she hadn't the comprehension or energy to explain the whole story and she really needed someone to help stop the panic.

Adrienne rounded the corner. "What's wrong?"

"We need to talk," she said, the trembling apparent in her voice. "Not here. Is the conference room around the corner vacant?"

Adrienne stepped out of the bathroom and it seemed like an eternity before she returned.

"Yes."

The two dashed to the conference room and Trisha crossed to the nearest seat, wrapped her hands around her waist and took a deep breath. "Oh, God, Adrienne. What am I going to do?"

Adrienne pulled a chair next to her and sat. "What happened?"

Trisha couldn't even say the words. The whole situation was too painful, too humiliating to even consider, much less seal it by actually saying it out loud. But she needed Adrienne. Adrienne would help her figure out what to do.

She squeezed her eyes shut and eked out the words. "I think Logan is Cyber Man."

She didn't open her eyes. She didn't want to see Adrienne's reaction. Would she laugh, be equally shocked or call the men in white coats to come take her away?

"No way."

"I think he is. I'm not sure. But I have a gut feeling. It's a bad feeling, Ade. I know I'm right."

She opened one eye in time to see Adrienne waving a hand in front of her face. "Whoa, back up. What happened?"

Trisha straightened in her seat, but she couldn't release the clench of her arms around her waist. It was the only thing holding her lunch in her stomach.

She took another breath, then another, before starting. "I heard him on the phone. Before he hung up, he told whoever he was talking to, 'Whenever you need me, I'm just a click away.'"

"Okay."

"That's the last thing Cyber Man says to me before we sign off. Every time, Ade. Every time, that's the last thing he says."

Now Adrienne was the one to take a deep breath. She placed her hands on the chair and squeezed, breathing deeply, obviously trying to let the comment sink in.

"That doesn't mean he's Cyber Man."

"Have you ever heard anyone use that phrase before?"

After an excruciatingly long pause, Adrienne replied, "No, but it's not an uncommon one. I mean, just because I've never heard anyone use it, doesn't mean other people don't. It's not like he said, 'Hikee-okee-eekee' or something equally strange."

Trisha turned her head and glared at her friend, wondering what the hell she was talking about.

"You know what I mean," Adrienne quipped. "'I'm just a click away.' That's not some far-out phrase that's beyond the realm of anyone other than Logan. It could just be coincidence."

"I have a feeling it's not. I can't explain it. I just…I just know it's him. I know it."

"Wait a minute. Let's consider this rationally. You and Logan ended up on the same Web site? What are the odds of that?"

Trisha had no idea, but they must have been steep.

Adrienne continued. "How did you find the site in the first place?"

Trisha traced her thoughts back in time and what she remembered didn't sit well.

"I found a brochure in the lobby downstairs. It was on the floor, like someone dropped it. I'd planned to toss it in the trash, but when I caught sight of the ad…well, it looked intriguing."

"You found it *downstairs?*"

"Ade, there's thousands of people in this building."

"Including Logan."

Fear swept through her.

"So what are you going to do?" Adrienne asked.

Trisha hadn't gotten that far. First, she needed to know she wasn't completely out of her mind, and the more she put the pieces together, the more real the horror became.

"Well…" she began, not sure how to finish. "I have to break it off with Cyber Man."

"So break it off. You were considering it anyway."

She was, before the personality-altering, mind-blowing orgasmathon of their last chat.

The transcript of their last session sped through her mind.

Their last session.

Oh, God, if that was Logan on the balcony… Oh, God, oh, God, oh, God.

She clamped her eyes shut, trying to erase the impact.

"Of course," Adrienne ventured, the tone in her voice telling Trisha she was about to spout a very crazy idea. "If it is Logan, you're in an interesting situation."

"What?"

"Think about this for a moment. You signed up with Cyber Man wanting a *replacement* for Logan. What if Cyber Man is Logan? The fantasy meets reality!"

"And I'll never be able to form a coherent sentence in front of the man again."

Adrienne huffed. "Trish, what do you want from life?"

For the moment Trisha allowed the confusion to drain from her thoughts as she considered the question. "I want a career that I enjoy. I want a husband that I love. I want children, a nice house in the hills. I want happily-ever-after."

"And if you could snap your fingers and make everything go your way, who would you have that with?"

The word came out in a whisper. "Logan."

"You've got a chance to get to know him, what he

really wants from love, what he really fears, underneath the facade."

A shot of heat blushed her cheeks.

Responding to Trisha's silence, Adrienne continued. "Trish, you have an opportunity to delve into his secrets, uncover his desires." She dropped her shoulders, apparently trying to find the right words. "Think of it this way. Think of Logan as a prospective client. You want his business. You want to beat out the competition and get straight to what the client wants. Without revealing your identity, you can draw out what he's looking for and use it to your advantage. It's no different than cooking up the perfect ad campaign."

Though Trisha didn't like her love life being compared to a sales pitch, she had to admit there was something behind Adrienne's idea. If Trisha got to know the real Logan Moore, one of two things could happen. She could either discover he wasn't the man for her and finally let him go completely, keeping her reputation intact, or she could get under his skin, find out what turned him on and use the information to creep up and snatch him.

"This could be the answer to my prayers," she said. Final resolution when it came to Logan Moore. "I can do this."

"Damn straight."

"I still don't know if it's him."

"Well," Adrienne said, leaning back in her seat. "What do you know about Cyber Man?"

Trisha stopped to consider. "He's a Pisces."

"Logan's a Pisces," Adrienne admitted. "March

eleventh. I remember because it's the same day as my mom's."

Trisha took a deep breath, trying to calm the jitters. "In the beginning, we gave each other descriptions, but nothing really specific. I know Cyber Man has dark hair, dark eyes and he said he's tall. That's it."

"That could certainly be Logan."

Trisha had no response. The thought that Pisces47 could really be Logan was beginning to sink in and it wasn't sitting well.

"Trish," Adrienne added, "It still might not be him, but if it is, I say go for it. It's your chance to discover the real Logan Moore."

The ache in Trisha's stomach eased as the situation unfolded in her mind. Adrienne was right. It was like gaining insider information. If she hated what she saw, she could let go of Logan once and for all. And if she liked what she saw, she could uncover what he wanted most from love, turn around and hand it to him on a silver platter.

She summed it all up in her mind and expressed her intentions with one short word.

"Shit."

BILL JEFFRIES sat in the Northern Winds Bookstore and Café fighting the urge to check his watch—again. Not only would it just be a painful reminder that time had seemingly stopped, but Adie had caught his gesture on several occasions and was now flashing him dirty looks.

He hadn't been able to find a solitary friend to accompany him to this poetry reading and he guessed that was probably a good thing. Anyone he would have coerced into coming along certainly wouldn't have remained a friend after suffering through this.

They'd been sitting in the dimly lit café for nearly an hour, but it seemed like forever, and as his gaze traveled over the hummus-eating crowd, all he could think about was tossing his iced tea, breaking out and heading for the first bar that offered a cold beer and a big-screen TV.

Trying to keep his eyes from his wrist, he glanced at the woman who was reading a poem on the small corner stage. With her horn-rimmed glasses and knee-high stockings, he might have pegged her as a nerd, but her sapphire-blue hair made a fashion statement he couldn't comprehend. She was reading something about oranges in the desert, and Bill hadn't a clue as to why poets couldn't just say what they meant in plain English.

In his opinion, poetry was useless if it didn't rhyme or begin with the phrase, "There once was a man from Nantucket…"

Normally, he enjoyed spending time with Adrienne's family. The Garfields' lifestyle was a refreshing change from his classic suburban upbringing and he always found their views interesting if not somewhat comical. Her father, Edward, held a doctorate in philosophy and her mother, Maya, had a masters in archaeology. But despite their credentials, the two had chosen a Bohemian lifestyle.

To look at them, you'd think they lived on the edge of poverty. Granted, Maya wore a collection of turquoise that could sustain a small Native American tribe for several years, but the two still sported around in their Vanagon, grew their own herbs and slept on a futon in their loft.

Even their kids had held on to their hippie ways, with Adrienne's sister, Robin, and her brothers, Winter and Storm, all looking as if they'd just returned from Woodstock. Only Adrienne attempted to break from the mold and infiltrate what her parents referred to as the eco-destroying mainstream.

As the baby of the family, Adrienne was the only one to have attended a public high school—the co-op her siblings had attended disbanded when she was twelve.

And Adrienne was more than eager to get a taste of life on the other side. She'd made friends—friends with televisions—and *Beverly Hills 90210* quickly became the guidebook that transformed Hummingbird Eucalyptus into Adrienne Garfield.

And it was a good thing for Bill. He questioned whether she would have caught his eye if she'd resembled the other women he was scanning right now. Most were a little too earthy for his liking. But he definitely liked the citified version of the flower child sitting across the table. Adrienne was as beautiful as her mother, but added touches of makeup and some style to her hair sent her over the edge into what Bill would classify as stunning abyss.

Though at the moment, her complexion seemed a little green.

He studied her for a moment, opened his mouth to ask if she was okay, but Edward interrupted.

"She's good, isn't she?"

"Huh?"

"Maya," Edward said, tilting his head toward the stage. Bill's thoughts had drifted so far, he hadn't even noticed Maya had taken the stage and was now spouting something about oppression in a country he'd never heard of.

"Yeah, great!" Bill lied.

A low, quiet chuckle seeped from Edward's chest. "Don't worry. I only half understand it myself, and I helped her write it."

"I'm not much for poetry," Bill confessed, taking another sip of his tea and wishing all the gods in heaven it was Scotch instead.

Edward's smile was warm and sincere. "You don't have to be, son. I know Maya appreciates you and Adie coming tonight."

A round of applause told Bill that Maya's poem had ended. As she stepped from the stage, a very rotund woman took the microphone and announced the readings had ended, bringing Bill a welcome sigh of relief. He mentally calculated the fewest amount of minutes he'd have to remain seated before he could politely rip Adrienne from her chair and get the hell out.

He darted his eyes to Adrienne as Maya took the seat next to her. Adie still looked ashen and he wondered what was wrong. Reaching over to take her hand, he asked, "You okay, hon?"

He could see her swallow hard through the curve of her throat. "Just a little queasy. Maybe it was the salad dressing from lunch."

Maya's face sobered with concern. She cupped Adrienne's jaw in her hand and looked her over closely.

"Mom, I'm—" Adrienne started, but a glowing smile came over Maya's face, halting her objection.

"Darling! You're pregnant. Why didn't you tell us?"

The iced tea Bill was about to swallow jutted north through his sinuses and left him choking for air.

And the look on Adrienne's face matched his own state of shock.

"I'm what?" she blurted.

"You're pregnant. You've got all the signs."

"She's guessing, right?" Bill squeaked after a sneeze.

"Mom, are you sure?"

Adrienne spoke to her mother as if the woman held a positive pregnancy test in her hand. Bill, on the other hand, grasped at the notion that this was just Maya's way of being funny.

"Of course, I am. Look at you." Maya was literally beaming. "You're pale, but you've got a flush to your cheeks." Her hand still cupping Adrienne's chin, she turned her face to the light. "Your eyes are puffy, your lips are pink. You've got the glow, sweetheart."

Maya turned to her husband. "Edward, we're going to be grandparents again!"

Edward rose and rounded the table, leaving Bill feeling desperately alone. He'd had plans for Edward. Edward was going to be Bill's voice of reason, the man who told him Maya was just pulling their leg, but Edward had deserted him, opting instead to give his daughter a warm congratulating hug, solidifying everyone's assumption that Maya was right.

As the group gathered around Adrienne, providing kisses and well wishes, Bill stared her down. Surely,

Adrienne would be the one sane person to fly over this cuckoo's nest and tell him this wasn't really happening.

Adrienne returned his stare, all right, but the look in her eyes didn't ease his anxiety. It fed it. She shot him a look of apology, shook her head as if to say she couldn't object, then shrugged her shoulders in acceptance of what she'd been told.

It was bad. Really bad. And as a swell threatened to close his throat, a clap to his back released it.

"So what do you think?" Edward asked, returning to his seat next to Bill. "You ready to be a father?"

Bill shook his head. "No."

The honest admission was met with a friendly laugh. "No one is, buddy."

"I think it's going to be a girl." Maya gushed. "What's your favorite bird?"

Adrienne's expression went flat. "A woodpecker."

Maya shrugged as if she thought that name might actually have promise.

"Adie's not going to name her baby Woodpecker, Mom," Robin said. "I'm guessing something nuclear, like Sally or Jean."

No way, Bill hadn't even choked down the notion of fatherhood and Ade's family was already naming the child. He shot her the most pleading look he could muster, using his eyes to beg her to leave.

"Look, Bill and I have to go," Adrienne said, not missing a beat. Bill nearly knocked the table over as he sprouted from his chair, ready to flee from this place in search of some semblance of sanity.

As Adrienne hugged her mother, Bill accepted

Edward's handshake, gave a shaky nod to the rest of her family then dashed from the store, leaving Adrienne stumbling behind in his grasp.

"So, she could be wrong about you, right?" Bill asked the moment the door closed behind them. "I mean, we've been using protection."

His own statement sent a chill up his spine. Who was he kidding? They used protection, unless the moment came rather suddenly and was packed with an extra dose of heat, which was most of the time.

"My mother's never wrong. She has a gift for that kind of thing."

"But it was dark in there. She'd just been on stage. It must have been frightening in front of all those people. She could be a little off."

The look on Adrienne's face told Bill the statement sounded as ridiculous to her as it had to him.

"My mother's never wrong," she repeated. "And...I am just a little late."

"You're late?!"

"Well, it's not that strange. I'm never on time."

Reality crept in. He felt it numb his toes then slowly rise to weaken his knees. It continued north, shriveling his manhood and filling his stomach on its way to do God knows what to his head.

"We...we..." he stuttered. "You need to see a doctor. You need to get checked out."

Adrienne scoffed. "Well, of course. I want to make sure the baby's healthy."

"So, you want to keep it?"

The level of shock on her face told Bill he may have

just stuttered himself into a big mess of trouble. He quickly tried to save his hide. "I mean, that's what I want if it's what you want."

Her features softened, easing *one* of Bill's current concerns.

"Look, Adrienne," he said, realizing they hadn't moved from the sidewalk. "Let's sit for a minute."

He glanced around and noticed a couple tables set up outside the bookstore. Leading her to a seat, he quickly waved off the server who had strolled in their direction. He didn't want to order drinks. He needed a minute to think. And once he collected his thoughts, he wasn't planning on drinking anything they served in the Northern Winds Bookstore.

"So," he said, rubbing his hand over hers. "How do you feel about this?"

She shrugged. "I don't know. How do you feel about this?"

Tension threatened to split his skull. "Oh, Adie, don't do this to me. I want to know what we should do."

"Well, jeez, Bill." She pulled her hand from his grasp. "I'm just as shocked as you. But, I guess I'm having a baby. There's not much else to do, is there?"

"So you'll go see a doctor tomorrow? I mean, before we get too excited, we should probably be sure."

"My mother's never wrong."

Bill's panic deepened as he felt their worlds collide. Where he came from, a woman wasn't pregnant unless a doctor said so, and despite Adrienne's beliefs, one glance in a dark café wasn't good enough to send him out for cigars.

"Adrienne, sweetie, you've got to see a doctor. We need to make sure everything's okay. You need to get one of those ultrasonic things."

She stared at the street and replied, "I can call first thing in the morning," then turned her eyes to Bill. "Besides, I know you won't believe any of this until someone in a white coat tells you it's true."

Busted.

He smiled, unsure if it looked caged or apologetic.

"I'll call Doctor Lana in the morning. She's a family friend. I'm sure she'll be able to take me right away."

Bill gently reached for Adrienne's face and gazed into her eyes for a very long time. His world had just spun around on its axis, and despite his shock and fear, he couldn't seem to muster any regret. Though he'd never spoken the words, he truly believed he was in love with Adrienne and through the speeding beat of his heart, a flash of excitement shot through.

He might actually be a father, and if he dug deep down, he had to admit, there wasn't a better woman to create a life with than the one in his hands. He brushed a thumb across her cheek.

"I love you, honey."

Adrienne opened her mouth, but hesitated to echo his words. Her jaw bobbed a bit before she finally said, "This is all a little shocking, isn't it?"

Not exactly the response he'd hoped for, but he had to admit a lot had just happened in a very short time.

He held his eyes on hers for another moment, trying to stifle his concerns over why she hadn't returned his sentiment. It wasn't every day Bill Jeffries told a woman he loved her and her dodged reaction wasn't what he'd expected.

He took a slow, calming breath. "Yes, it is," he said. "And it will all turn out fine."

He pressed his lips to her forehead and silently prayed that would be true.

5

Daily Love Horoscope for Scorpio

Today brings opportunity to clear the mystery
that has shrouded your love life for quite some
time. But when you do, will you like what you
find? Only your heart can answer that question.

"WHERE DO YOU WANT to go tonight, baby?"

Trisha stared at the words she'd seen so many times
before, but tonight, fixed on the notion that this could
be Logan Moore, the question shot a jolt of adrenaline
through her that shook every nerve in her body.

She focused on the task at hand. She needed to
know if Pisces47 was really her boss and tonight was
the night to do it. She'd left work early, getting home
in time to go through the transcripts of all their chats
and the situation remained the same. Pisces47 had
provided very little information about himself, but
the information he had provided continued to support
the fact that the man on the other end could indeed be
Logan Moore.

It all fit Logan right down to the couch he'd mentioned in his office, but the sum of the parts still wasn't enough to tell her for sure. In the next few minutes, she would coax him into providing something solid. She had a plan for how to do it, but how she would feel when she got her answer, she wasn't sure.

She gave herself one last chance to back away and end it now, but decided she needed an answer, so, despite the tremors in her fingers, she raised a hand to the keyboard and opted to proceed.

"The beach was fun, but we have to go back to work now."

"Work is play when you're around, honey."

The thought of those words coming from Logan brought a new intensity to everything she read and for the first time she realized she really had been in tune to the idea that Pisces47 was just a pimply teenager.

She took a breath and continued. "We're back at the office, but I can't forget making love to you on the balcony, from behind."

"Mmm, it was memorable."

"I'm thinking about the couch in your office. You said it was under a window."

"I'm all over it, baby."

"It's been a long day. I kick off my shoes and kneel on your couch. I'm gazing out the window, admiring the view."

"And so am I. You've bent over the couch. Your ass is teasing me, begging me to caress my hand over those luscious cheeks."

This couldn't really be Logan, she thought. The man never used words like ass, but then again, it wasn't the type of thing that came up in normal business discussions.

She pushed away her doubts and continued to pursue her goal.

"I feel your warm hands come up under my skirt. You groan when you realize I'm naked underneath. Your hands clamp to my hips and pull me against your groin. You want me to feel the stiffness, and the hardness makes me wet." She touched the mouse and clicked Send.

"You part your legs for me, allowing me access to that sweet, slippery spot between your thighs. I lift your blouse, so I can run my tongue along your spine while I pleasure you with my hands."

The sharp stab to her chest told her this would be harder than she thought.

She took another breath and began to type.

"You're turning me on, Pisces. Your fingers are warm, they're sliding between my thighs, stroking my most sensitive spot. I gaze out the window and watch the scenery as pleasure boils in my veins."

Okay, here goes.

"Tell me, Pisces, what do I see?"

She raised a hand to the mouse and clicked Send, then held her breath and waited for an answer. Would it be a desert, green fields, something telling her this wasn't Logan Moore's office?

Time seemed to stop as she waited for the words to pop on the screen.

"You see bright crystals of light, sparkling off the water."

The bay. Is it San Francisco Bay?

The need for answers burned off the last of her doubts and filled her with a sense of urgency.

Her fingers sped over the keyboard. "Is it an ocean, a clear blue ocean?" With a quick move, she clicked Send.

Sweat beaded on her forehead and she raised a shaky hand to brush it away as seconds ticked by like hours. She waited for him to respond, her toes tapping wildly on the floor, shaking her chair and jiggling the keyboard in her hands.

He was taking forever. Why was he taking forever?

"It's whatever you want it to be, baby."

No! Just answer the question!

She took a deep breath.

She had to calm down.

She couldn't afford mistakes, so she took a moment and forced herself to relax.

Her anxiousness eased, she closed her eyes and slowly began to type. "I want our fantasy to be real for you. I want to see what you see in your office, when you're thinking of me."

There was a long pause that did horrible things to the rate of her pulse. She needed him to play along. She needed to know if this was really Logan Moore and short of this approach, she knew no other way to get the answer to her question.

"Through the buildings, you see a bay. The water is cold and choppy, but my hands are warm and smooth. Cars glide over the bridge, like my fingers glide between your folds."

Oh, God. The Bay bridge.

His words continued to roll over the screen. "There's a building across the street. You press your hands to the cool glass as the heat builds between your legs. You wonder if the people outside can see you."

"Can they, Pisces? Are there people outside?"

Her hands shook as she waited for his answer.

"No, we're high. But there's a building across the street. You wonder if people can see you, pressed against the glass, but a sweep of my finger rips your thoughts away. Your breath is going heavy, soft moans creep up your throat. You're nearly ready for me, aren't you, Scorpio?"

Trisha didn't even see the question. Her eyes were still planted on the description Pisces provided, a description that nailed the view outside Logan's office.

She stopped breathing. Images began to rush through her mind, mixed with a fear over what she should do. She was nearly certain this was Logan Moore, and though the whole idea seemed good at the time, now she wasn't sure she should continue the online chat.

She wasn't sure she could.

"Are you ready, Scorpio?"

The movement on the screen caught her attention. She was freezing up, about to blow this session and everything she'd managed to accomplish so far.

Quickly, she reached for the keyboard and began typing whatever came to her mind. "Yes, yes. You've got me hot, Pisces. So hot for you. I want your hard length between my legs. I want you inside. Deep inside, like you were before." She reached for the mouse and clicked Send.

"I release my trousers and brush my cock between your legs. You're so slick and I'm so hard. I want to take you again, Scorpio. Like on the balcony. I yank at your hips and pull you against me. You have to grip the couch and hold on. Your palms are moist and the cool leather slips from your grasp."

A leather couch.

This was Logan. This was really Logan. And suddenly she didn't know if the heat in her cheeks was from embarrassment or desire.

She kept him going. "Take me, please. I need you."

Lame, but it was all her muddled thoughts would provide.

"I guide the tip to your entrance and in one fierce stroke, thrust up. You want to cry out in pleasure, but you can't, so your groan locks in your throat. I'm taking you hard and fast, and you bend, wanting me deeper, wanting more.

"I thrust farther while my fingers reach around and tease your clit. I want you to come, like you did on the balcony. I want your release to massage me and make me burst."

The words seemed to sting her eyes. She was still in denial, unable to believe the man talking sexy on the screen was really the cool, reserved man she lusted over every day.

She needed more. She needed to remove all possibility of coincidence from her mind. After all, there were thousands of offices in San Francisco's financial district, thousands of men who could possibly fit the description he'd provided. And for all she knew, there could be dozens of other cities built along a bay, with a bridge that spanned choppy gray waters.

She jumped in with one last idea. "I turn my head and press my cheek to the cool glass. I'm about to go over, but I want to last longer, I'm trying to hold on. I open my eyes. I'm looking for something to fix my eyes on. What can I fix my eyes on?"

There was a long pause. She was taking this too far and now the trembling in her hands came from fear that she'd just played one too many cards. Any moment, she expected a question to pop on the screen, asking her what the hell she was doing.

What she got instead stopped her heart completely. "Horses. Wild bronze horses. They're running in a team and the freedom they portray matches the freedom you feel when you burst in release."

She stared at the screen, unable to move. Any shred of doubt she may have been holding evaporated when Pisces47 described Logan's bronze Remington statue.

This was it. This was really it.

She was having cybersex with Logan Moore.

Her throat slammed shut and she gulped, trying to clear a passage and take in air. She would have fled from the computer but she was paralyzed by all the questions spinning through her mind, the most prominent being, "Why?"

Logan could have any woman in San Francisco. What was he doing on the Internet, sharing fantasies with a stranger?

"I'm ready to come, Scorpio. Come with me, baby."

Her eyes froze on the words as if they were suddenly toxic. How could she do this? How could she possibly do this, knowing it was Logan on the other end?

And how could she ever look the man in the eye again?

"Are you ready, Scorpio?"

Get it together, Trish!

She had plenty of time to sort this out later. Right now, she had to get a grip and get on track before she blew it.

Her mind barely capable of rational thought, she raised her hand to the keyboard and typed, "urd," then reached for the mouse, nearly clicking the button before she noticed what she'd done.

"Aagh!" She slammed her finger over the backspace key, replaced the jabber with "yes" and clicked Send.

His words filled the screen but she could no longer make sense of them. She didn't want the fantasy. She didn't want to play this out. Not tonight. She'd thought she was prepared, but now that the truth was firmly in front of her, she realized it wasn't so.

She watched as he played out the climax, each word bringing a new level of heat to her cheeks until the climactic end hit her like an inferno.

She refused to let any of it happen in her mind. She couldn't afford that level of intimacy at the moment. Instead, she skimmed the text, looking for a signal that she would be required to reply.

"How do you feel, Scorpio?"

How did she feel? Several words came to mind, "mortified" being the one that seemed most fitting.

She raised her fingers to the keyboard and lied.

"Good."

His normal response was, "Me, too," but tonight there was nothing. Just a long, nerve-splitting wait that made her wonder how much damage she'd just done. She had no idea how she'd come across tonight, and as seconds ticked by, she became more and more nervous over what she might have said.

"You aren't yourself tonight, Scorpio. Is everything okay?"

She had blown it. She'd crossed the line and raised suspicion. She shouldn't have done this. She should have simply ended the relationship when she suspected it was Logan. But she didn't. She'd decided to play a game and now she was stuck, wondering what the hell she should do.

"What you do," she said to herself, "is pull yourself together and stop acting like a timid little mouse."

She stared at the screen, allowing her own words to sink in and provide the reassurance she needed. She had to finish what she'd started. Adrienne had been right. This was no different than gaining some valuable information to land a prized account and if she could do it for her job, she could do it for her love life.

She took a deep, cleansing breath and raised her hands to the keyboard. "I'm just tired tonight. I've had a long day."

"Scorpio, don't ever feel you need to chat if you aren't up to it, honey."

His words stung deep in her chest. The man she knew as Pisces definitely wasn't the playboy she'd seen at work. Maybe Adrienne was right, that his fetish for light affairs was just a post-divorce phase. Pisces had always expressed appreciation for her thoughts and wit, which didn't fit with Logan's preference for air-headed bimbos.

So who was the real man inside, Pisces or Logan?

She typed her response. "I'm always up for our chats, but now I'd like to rest. Will you rest on the couch with me for a while? Do you have to go?"

"I can always make time for you, baby. Spread out next to me, rest your head on my shoulder and tell me about your day."

Oh, if she only could.

"I'd rather just put it behind me. But I was wondering if I could ask you a question. Something personal."

"Sure."

She rubbed her hands over her thighs, considered one last time, then took a deep breath and went on.

"Why do you do this? Why do you make love to someone you can't touch?"

Her words hung on the screen, unanswered, reviving those fears she thought she'd overcome.

She quickly added, "I'm sorry. You don't have to answer that."

"I don't mind. It's a question I've asked myself many times." There was a pause before he went on. "It's not always easy to find love with the people around me."

"Are you looking for love?"

Again she waited for the answer as the blank screen stared back at her, echoing silence on the other end of the line. She raised her fingers to the keyboard, ready to tell him he didn't need to answer, when the words finally rolled onto the screen.

"It's not as simple as finding love. I need something deeper than that, something that goes far beyond just being in love. The love part's easy, it's the rest that's hard to find."

"What more is there than love?"

"Trust."

That one word stared back at her, draining all her fear and apprehension to make way for a single, overwhelming emotion.

Guilt.

The man of her fantasies had just divulged his innermost need, and it was the one thing she had just betrayed. She cringed at the irony. She'd wanted to find out what he wanted most in life, what he needed in a lover, and to do it, she'd gone behind his back, betrayed his trust, only to find out that trust was what he most desired.

She placed her fingers on the keys and typed, "I'm sorry you don't feel you have someone you can trust."

But he did. He could trust her. Even though her actions didn't display it.

"What about you, Scorpio? Why do you do this?"

She thought for a moment and decided it was time to be as truthful as possible.

"I can't have the man I want."

"Is he married?"

"No. He's simply off-limits."

It took him a long time to respond and she realized her comment could have been construed a million different ways. But at least it was honest, and if she couldn't reveal her identity to Pisces47, she would at least tell the truth whenever she could.

"I'm sorry, Scorpio, but I'll be here for you. Whenever you need me, I'm just a click away."

LOGAN STARED out the window of his office wondering how the hell his entire staff had managed to fall apart over the course of one day.

Something had happened to turn Bill into a bungling rubble of nerves, but the man wasn't breathing a word of explanation. After practically mowing Logan over to answer the phone, he'd promptly bit the head off the supplier who had called, then rushed out of the office muttering something about explaining later.

The Bradley campaign had come to a screeching halt waiting for Adrienne to sign off on the final graphics, but the woman was nowhere to be found. Sylvia had only said Adrienne had an appointment and she'd be in soon, but as each moment ticked by without her, the chances of delivering the final mock-ups on time were dwindling down to slim and none.

And if that wasn't bad enough, the nerves that had Trisha on edge for the past few weeks had seemingly returned, leaving Logan wondering if the leak about her promotion had made it to her own ears.

Trisha had just begun to relax about the Tyndale campaign. Things were returning to normal and he had to blow it by discussing his intention with Human Resources. If word had gotten back to Trisha, she was surely feeling the weight of the pressure.

He exhaled the breath he'd been holding, leaned over the deep sill of the window and gazed at the city below. He thought about Trisha, and for a moment, allowed his mind to go places it had no business going. It trailed over her long silken legs, slid over her soft auburn hair and kissed those full pink lips, wandering over her body and mentally exploring every curve and crevice he'd long ago banned from his thoughts.

Logan rarely let his mind go there, but to refuse was getting harder and harder each day and he wondered if he was truly as controlled as he'd like to believe.

Could he be sending the wrong signals to Trisha? He'd tried not to, but on more than one occasion he thought she'd caught his eyes on places they didn't belong.

And if she suspected his interest in her then heard of the promotion, Lord knew what she could be thinking.

"Logan?"

He turned at the sound of Trisha's voice. Locking eyes with hers, a trickling bead of sweat touched his brow, causing him to worry.

"I'm sorry. I didn't mean to interrupt you."

He opened his mouth to speak when his personal assistant, Kelly, popped her head in the office.

"The proofs are being couriered to Bradley right now," she said.

He blinked and brought his attention back to business.

"Adrienne squared away the graphics?"

"She just got in and printed off the final revision. Colin should be receiving them in the hour."

He relaxed his stance and moved back to his desk. Thank heaven for small favors. That was at least one thing he could get off his mind today.

"Thanks for letting me know."

Trisha took two small steps into his office as Kelly returned to her desk. Trisha's smile was pleasant, but the perk in her expression was clearly forced. She was obviously trying hard to put up a casual front, and Logan wished again he could go back in time and do things differently.

"I just wanted to let you know I sent you a link to the proposed Web site for Cape Horn."

He cleared his throat and took a seat at his desk. "Let's take a look," he said, scrolling through his e-mails. "How did it turn out?"

"It's good. I think you'll like it."

He clicked on the URL to bring the Web site into view.

"Hey, this is great. I like the tone and the colors. It goes well with the new image we're trying to portray."

"I like it, too," she said. "We don't have all the links working, but we wanted to get your initial thoughts before we moved on."

"Let's go with it."

"Great," Trisha said. She took a step back and bumped straight into Bill.

"Good, you're both here. We can tell you together," Bill said as he stepped into the office with Adrienne trailing behind him.

The two had wide grins plastered on their faces, raising Logan's curiosity. He'd known something was up with Bill and was pleased to see whatever it was, it was apparently something good.

They moved into the office as Bill closed the door, deepening Logan's wonder. The cautious smile on Trisha's face told him she was equally confused.

Bill took Adrienne's hand, inhaled a deep breath then let it out in a huff. "So, we've got news," he said, overstating the obvious.

Logan couldn't imagine what this was about. Bill and Adrienne hadn't been working on any projects together, so he doubted it was business. But at the same time, they hadn't been dating long, either, so anything on the personal side seemed out of the question, as well.

In typical fashion, Bill stood for a moment, grinning, dragging the moment out and causing Logan to raise his hands and ask, "Well?"

Bill took another breath then exhaled, "Adie's pregnant. We're having a baby."

The statement hit Logan like a punch in the stomach. That was the last thing he'd expected to hear and given the circumstances of their relationship, he had no idea whether congratulations or condolences were in order.

Not knowing how to respond, he darted his eyes to Trisha, deciding this was one of those times where it would be wise to follow a woman's lead.

"Oh, my God!" Trisha exclaimed. "So...are you guys happy about this? I mean, is this a good thing?"

The honest approach. It would have been his last choice, but it seemed to be going over well.

"Frankly," Adrienne said, "we didn't plan it, but yeah, we're pretty happy."

Trisha wrapped her arms around Adrienne as Logan rounded his desk to give Bill a firm handshake.

"Congratulations," he said, pressing a kiss to Adrienne's cheek. He stuttered and shook his head. "I'm…I'm stunned. I'm not sure what to say."

Bill and Adrienne laughed. "We were, too," Bill said. "But it's sinking in and we're excited."

"Well, I'm happy for you. This is wonderful."

Adrienne turned to Trisha. "So, we wanted to keep this quiet around the office." She glanced at Logan. "You two are the only ones who know."

"Of course," Trisha agreed.

"I'm just over four weeks along, which is still in the touchy stage. We'll give it a couple months and let you know when we're ready for publicity."

Logan smiled. "Your secret's safe with me."

Adrienne released a quick breath. "I'm behind on a few things, so I really need to get back to my office. We just wanted to break the news."

"Actually," Trisha said, following her to the door, "I'm right behind you." She turned to Logan. "So Cape Horn's a go?"

"Yes, absolutely," Logan said, returning to his desk.

Trisha followed Adrienne out the door as Bill took a seat at Logan's desk.

"So this is what had you climbing the walls this morning?"

Bill still looked giddy. Logan would have never thought the man would be this enthused about being a father. Bill had always been happy enjoying his free-dom and Logan wondered if the man truly knew what was in store for him.

"I'm sorry, man. Adie and I agreed to keep quiet until she got checked out by the doctor this morning."

"And you're really happy about this? I mean, you two haven't been dating long."

Bill frowned. "It's not like she's a stranger. We've known each other for a few years now."

Logan felt a pang of regret. He hadn't meant to rain on Bill's parade. He just hadn't realized their relation-ship had grown so serious.

"Hey, I'm happy if you're happy. I didn't see this coming, that's all."

Bill eased his frown and chuckled. "Tell me about it. I didn't, either, and trust me, I had my share of belts last night after Adie's mom dropped the bomb." He shook his head and laughed. "That woman's amazing. She took one look at Adie and told us she was pregnant. I didn't believe her, but she apparently knew what she was talking about. The doctor confirmed it this morning."

"So where's she having the baby?"

"U.C.S.F., I guess. That's where the doctor's affiliated."

"That's a top-notch facility."

"You bet. I'm not settling for anything but the best when it comes to my kid. I want to make sure every-thing goes smooth as silk."

Logan tilted his chair back and smiled. Bill was truly beaming and the side of him he'd buried years ago was actually jealous that it was Bill starting a family and not him. If things had turned out the way he'd believed, he would have had a few children of his own right now.

"Hey, I was wondering," Bill said. "I want to buy Adie a ring. Go with me? You've got better taste than me and I want it to be perfect."

Logan's eyes went wide. "You asked her to marry you?"

"Not yet, but I plan to."

"Don't you think you're rushing things?"

The sour frown returned to Bill's face, but this time Logan didn't feel any regret. Bill was clearly getting carried away here and he couldn't help but feel the man was moving too fast.

"She's the mother of my child," Bill said in defense. "And besides, I'm in love with her. Under the circumstances, marriage seems like a pretty natural move to me."

"You're in love? You never mentioned that before."

"It's not exactly something that comes up on the basketball court." Bill winked. "I'm usually too busy kicking your ass."

Logan shrugged. "Sure, I'll go with you, but I don't see what's the hurry. Why not let the pregnancy sink in a bit before you start planning a wedding? That's a lot to deal with all at once."

"You just hate weddings."

"I do," Logan replied, chuckling at the pun.

Bill laughed along with him. "Well, don't worry, pal. This one ain't yours."

Logan looked at his watch. "I'm free this afternoon. I've got a few things to take care of, then we could cut out for a couple hours. How does that sound?"

"Like a plan."

Bill rose from his chair and stepped to the door.

"Hey, Bill," Logan said, causing Bill to stop and turn. "I'm really happy for you."

Bill replied with another wink. "It's all good, buddy."

6

"OKAY, how do you really feel?"

Trisha set her elbows on the wood-laminate table at Yasuda's Restaurant and laced her hands together, waiting for Adrienne to answer her question. The two had left Logan's office, grabbed their purses and headed out the door, deciding business could wait. Too many things had happened in the last twenty-four hours and the women were in dire need of a major regroup.

Adrienne blew a quick breath toward her bangs, causing the fluffy yellow tresses to flutter in the air before settling back down over her eyes.

"Honestly? Between Bill and my family, I haven't had a chance to grasp how I feel. They've all swarmed on me like vultures to the point where I'm ready to scream and I've known about this for…what—" she looked at her watch "—less than twenty-four hours?"

Trisha flashed an apologetic smile. "I'm sorry. I'm sure everyone's excited, that's all."

"I just wish I could have found out on my own before everyone started hovering."

The server approached their table with two steaming cups of hot-and-sour soup then quickly scurried away.

It was one of the reasons Yasuda's had become their favorite restaurant when the women wanted to talk. Unlike other restaurants in the Financial District, the waiters didn't hang around and chitchat, and the walled-in booths offered the utmost privacy.

"My mother's called four times," Adrienne continued. "She's got supplements and a special diet plan I'm supposed to follow. She's already contacted the midwife and crossed the beach house off everyone's vacation list within a month of my due date."

"You aren't seriously going to have your baby at the beach house."

Adrienne raised her hands at her sides, clearly frustrated. "See? This is exactly what I mean. I have no idea. My parents just assume that's the way the birth will be handled. No one's asking my opinion about anything. And I don't even want to *think* how Bill would react if I suggested not having the baby in a hospital. He wouldn't even believe I was pregnant until I got a blood test from Dr. Lana."

She huffed and plopped back against the red-vinyl booth.

"You should have seen him. The moment I told him Dr. Lana worked at U.C. San Francisco, he assumed that's where I'd have the baby. He went on and on about their high-tech facilities, how they're prepared to handle even the most extreme complications. The way he talks, you'd think I was having brain surgery instead of a baby."

She shook her head, picked up the porcelain spoon and began stirring her soup.

"I'm ready to run away and I just found out about

this last night. The only good thing that's happened so far is that Bill agreed not to tell his parents until I'm further along. I couldn't handle them thrown in the mix right now. This will be their first grandchild, you know."

Trisha sighed in sympathy for her friend. "I'm sorry, Ade. I'm sure everything will settle down. Everyone's just over the moon right now."

The two sipped their soup in silence. Though Trisha understood Adrienne being overwhelmed by her situation, she could tell there was more behind her friend's mood than what she'd been told.

Trisha raised the spoon to her lips and casually added, "Bill sure seems happy about it."

Adrienne's flinch told Trisha she'd hit a nerve. She set the spoon on the table. "What is it, Ade? What's the real deal with you and Bill?"

Adrienne lifted the cup to her lips and muttered from the rim, "He told me he loved me."

A smile worked its way up Trisha's chest and threatened to emerge, but Adrienne's less-than-enthusiastic expression stopped it short.

"What's wrong with that?" Trisha asked. "You're crazy about Bill. I would have thought that would make you happy, especially given the situation."

Adrienne set down the cup a little too forcefully and pointed a finger toward Trisha. "Exactly," she said. "Given the situation."

"I don't get it."

"He never breathed a word about love before he thought I was pregnant. How do I know he's not simply caught up in the moment?"

"Oh, Ade. I'm sure Bill wouldn't have told you he loved you if he didn't mean it."

"His timing stunk."

"But, Adrienne, you can't think—"

Adrienne pushed the cup away and dropped back in her seat. "Exactly, I can't think. I can't think about anything. I've been handed the shock of my life, my hormones have been in turmoil for over a week—and now I know why. I've got my parents hanging around me like a pack of hyenas, planning every detail of my pregnancy and Bill wandering around so bubbly it's creepy."

She sighed and placed her face in her palms. "I need everyone to take a giant breather, back off and leave me alone for thirty seconds so I can figure out what I'm going to do."

Trisha pushed her soup bowl to the edge of the table and took a hand from Adrienne's face. "Adie, they will. Just give everyone time to calm down and in the meantime, go home, unplug the phone, lock your doors and take a long, warm, uninterrupted bath. Put on some soft music and treat yourself to a soothing cup of tea."

"You're right."

"You're overwhelmed. Everyone is. Don't jump all over Bill for saying he loves you. I, for one, happen to think he's sincere."

"I think he's confused."

"Well, you two will have plenty of time to sort that out. Get yourself in order first. Take some time off if you need it. I'm sure Logan wouldn't mind."

The budding smile drained from Adrienne's face.

"God, Trisha, I completely forgot! Your chat last night. What did you find out?"

The reminder dampened Trisha's good mood. Adrienne's news had caused her to all but forget about her *chat* with Logan and the situation she now faced.

The server approached their table with two bowls of steamed rice and trays of teriyaki chicken breast, giving Trisha an opportunity to casually peek around the paper partition to ensure no one they knew had taken a seat behind them. The booth was thankfully empty.

She glanced at Adrienne, pausing a moment for the lanky man to shuffle out of earshot.

"Pisces, Cyber Man, pimply-face kid...it's Logan."

Adrienne's mouth dropped open. "Are you sure?"

Trisha nodded. "I got him to describe his office, the view out the window, his leather couch. There's no doubt." Just talking about it brought back the jitters. "He even described the Remington on his credenza."

Adrienne shook her head. "I almost can't believe it. I mean, what are the odds of something like this happening?"

"There have to be thousands of people signed up to that site."

"Aunt Margaret would say it's fate."

"And for once, I'd agree with your crazy aunt."

Adrienne stared at her rice, stabbing the starchy granules with her chopsticks, but not yet taking a bite. The ashen tone of her face told Trisha she was probably done eating.

"Are you okay?"

"Yeah," Adrienne said, chuckling. "For days I thought I was coming down with a bug." She pushed the food away and reached for her tea. "So, what did you do?" she asked.

Trisha blew out a bitter huff. "I got him to tell me why he's doing it. The cybersex thing." She picked up her chopsticks and began digging into her rice. Unlike Adrienne, who rarely ate to excess, Trisha always sought comfort in food, and given her current situation, she needed all the comfort she could gather.

"And?" Adrienne asked.

"He's got major issues with trust." She took a bite of rice and added, "And how did I find that out? By lying to him."

"Oh, come on, Trisha. You're being too hard on yourself. How could you have told him about Scorpio? I mean, think about it. You weren't even sure until last night during your chat."

"I should have done something when I first suspected."

Adrienne snorted and took another short sip of her tea. "What were you supposed to do? Say, 'Hey Logan, you sound like the guy I'm having computer sex with'?"

"I could have ended it."

"So end it now."

Logical statement. A mountain of rationality behind it. And Trisha had no intention of following the sound advice. She was in a position to be intimate with the man of her dreams and now that she'd come this far, she wasn't going to turn back.

"I can't," she finally replied.

"Why not?"

Trisha was afraid of that question, and more afraid of the response she'd get when she answered. Adrienne had always been the savvy half of the pair when it came to sexual relationships and she knew her answer was going to sound gullible and stupid, but there was no way around giving it straight. Besides, maybe she needed to have some sense knocked into her before the whole thing blew up in her face.

"He needs me," she answered, then quickly winced, awaiting the expected response.

"He needs you."

There it was. That deadpan tone Adrienne reserved for when someone tried to feed her a line of bull. The last time she'd heard it was at Quincy's when a supposed eligible bachelor tried to explain the tan line on his wedding finger.

Trisha took a breath and sighed. "I spent the night reading through all our chats. He's no playboy."

"I told you that was just a post-divorce phase."

"He's vulnerable. He's been hurt. And I know for a fact that Scorpio is all he has right now. I can't abandon him now."

Her wince deepened to the point where she was nearly crouching in the booth, waiting for Adrienne's uproarious laugher to tell her she was a complete idiot.

"You believe that?"

Ouch, that stung. Trisha would have rather received the laughs than the "you're pathetic" sound of that response. But despite Adrienne's disbelief, Trisha knew she was right. She had a sixth sense when it came to

people. It was one of the reasons she was so success-
ful at her job. She had an uncanny ability to disregard
a person's words for the subtleties that lay beneath
them, and Logan Moore was no exception.

She mustered the courage to look Adrienne in the
eye. "I can feel it. And you know how dead-on I am
when I get a feeling."

Adrienne conceded with a nod as she hesitantly slid
the bowl of rice in front of her, topped it with some soy
sauce and readied her chopsticks.

"So, you set out to learn something about our mys-
terious boss. What have you learned so far?"

"That trust is more important to him than love and if
I want him, I have to earn his trust. But how can I do that
if I'm deceiving him about the identity of Scorpio63? I
mean, even if I came clean right now, how do I know he
wouldn't fire me on the spot? How could he work with
me knowing I'm the one he's been cyberscrewing?"

"You're dealing with it."

"Barely. And it's different for him. He owns the
company. He's in a position of authority." She took
another bite of her rice and shook her head. "I'm not
sure that he'd keep me on board if he knew I was
Scorpio. I mean, some of those chats…"

She trailed off as the memory of their sex on the
balcony played over in her mind. How would he react
if he knew that was her? With embarrassment or in-
trigue? He'd most definitely see her in a new light, but
whether it would be a good light or bad, she had no idea.

"Look," Adrienne said. "The way I see it, you've got
two options. You make up some excuse to end the

online chats and keep the secret to yourself. Put it all in the past and move on."

That would be the smart thing to do, but just the notion brought a swell of regret to Trisha's stomach. She didn't want to lose Pisces, for herself as much as for him. She'd developed affection for the man that multiplied a thousand times when she found out it was Logan Moore. She had a window to his heart, a way to dig in and share the part of the man she always knew was under the surface. To walk away now would be to let it all go and she wasn't ready to let go just yet.

"What's my other option?"

"Keep playing along and see where it takes you."

"I like that option."

"It's dangerous."

"It was your idea."

"I never said it was a good idea."

Trisha raised an eyebrow. "So, now you're changing your tune?"

Adrienne was about to take another bite of rice, but the question stopped her in her tracks. "One wrong move, one slip-up and you've blown it all. Is it really worth the risk?"

It was a good question. One Trisha couldn't answer.

Adrienne went on. "You're playing with fire. If it were me, I'd break it off with Pisces, keep the secret to myself and concentrate on my job. If you want Logan, get him the old fashioned way, up front and in person."

"Ade, he's my boss. This isn't like you and Bill. I can't just go propositioning the man I report to, at least, not without some certainty that he's interested. If I keep the chats up, I might find a way to feel him out, to see what he thinks about dating women at the office. Using Scorpio, I can do that anonymously and get a sense of my options before I make a move that could be disastrous."

"Are you sure?"

Trisha wasn't sure of anything other than the more she chatted with Pisces, the more she wanted the man behind the screen and the thought of letting him go was too much to bear.

"Some things are worth taking a risk," she finally said.

"Well," Adrienne offered, "I hope you know what you're doing."

LOGAN HAD JUST RETURNED from the pitch at Tyndale headquarters when Kelly stopped by his office. "Virginia Matthews is holding for you. She's called several times."

The announcement brought a smile to his face. The fact that Virginia was so anxious to talk to him could only be a good sign, and after the job Trisha had done, Logan knew Virginia had cause for worry.

Every question Marc Tyndale presented, Trisha had answered with razor-sharp precision that seemed to heighten his interest, and his confidence, in the Moore Agency. By the time she'd finished her presentation, Marc was clearly impressed.

And so was Logan.

Trisha had played every note perfectly, from her enthusiasm about the campaign, to her knowledge of the industry, right down to the conservative pale blue suit she'd worn for the meeting. It had been a perfect contrast to the flaming red cocktail dresses Virginia typically flaunted around in.

Virginia was of the opinion that the fewer clothes she wore, the better chance she had at landing the account and in some cases, it worked. Even Marc Tyndale had bought her notion that sex sells, and the campaign worked well for a while. But Marc was going through a change in life, a change that had prompted him to take a second look at the image of Tyndale Resorts and the direction he was going in was sure to leave Virginia Matthews in the dust.

And Trisha Bain was the perfect candidate to take the wheel and drive Marc back to the Moore Agency where he belonged.

"Thank you, Kelly. I'll take the call. Please close the door on your way out."

He waited for the click of the door then picked up the receiver. "Virginia, to what do I owe this pleasure?"

"Don't be coy with me."

Logan smiled. Virginia's voice was tainted with just enough anger to let him know she was running scared. Marc must have called her the moment they'd left his office, which was even better than he expected. He'd thought surely Marc would have wanted to think it over for a day or two. Apparently, his mind was made up.

"I take it you've heard from Marc," he said.

Her voice stilled, but he could hear the traces of anger seeping through. "Don't get too excited yet, darling. I'm ten steps ahead of you, as always."

The smile faded from his lips. "Pardon me?"

"We've already restructured the Tyndale ads. He'll be seeing his new campaign tomorrow. I just thought I'd let you know that you haven't won." Her tone shifted from anger to sarcasm. "I wouldn't want you to waste a good bottle of champagne for nothing."

His blood began to boil as his hand clamped tightly to the phone. Marc hadn't said anything about reviewing new campaigns from the Matthews Agency, or any other advertising firms for that matter. He'd all but given them the green light to proceed and Logan suddenly wondered if he was being played for a pawn.

He took a silent breath, released the tight grip on his jaw and forced a casual tone. Virginia was calling for no other reason than to make him squirm and he wouldn't give her the satisfaction.

"I wish you luck, Ginny," he said, trying to remain above her level.

"No, Logan, I don't need your luck to hold on to Tyndale. He's already mine, so I suggest you go back to your Puffy Cream Doughnuts and leave the high-end accounts to me."

He bit back a curse, reminding himself that annoying people was one of Virginia's favorite pastimes. She could only get to him if he let her and he wasn't going to let her.

"We'll just have to see what Tyndale thinks of your new ads."

"I already know what he'll think. I just wanted to be the first to tell you you've lost again, sweet cheeks."

"Don't be so sure of yourself. You've heard that old saying about counting your chickens before they've hatched. You end up with egg on your face."

The next thing he heard was a dial tone, which was just as well. Two more minutes on the phone with Virginia would have reduced him to personal attacks and he wasn't going to allow the woman to bring out the worst in him.

He pressed a finger to the receiver, tempted to dial Marc to ask why he hadn't mentioned the meeting with Virginia, but he chose to set down the phone instead. Any call to Marc at this point would come across as desperate and concerned and he was neither.

Marc said a day or two, and a day or two he could wait.

TRISHA STEPPED into her office, surprised to see Logan standing over her ads for the Cape Horn resort.

"Did you hear from Marc?" she asked.

He looked up and met her gaze. He'd lost the sparkle of victory that had set in his eyes the moment they'd left Tyndale's office and she was suddenly riddled with fear. Tyndale couldn't have turned them down. Of all the accounts she'd gone after, she was more certain about this than any.

"No, but I heard from Virginia Matthews. Her agency has apparently come up with a new campaign that Marc will be reviewing tomorrow."

Relief settled into her shoulders, breaking the tension that had spun up the back of her neck. She stepped to her desk and set down the artwork she'd collected from the graphics department.

"Well, that's a relief. By the look on your face, I thought Marc had nixed the campaign."

Logan didn't answer. He simply resumed mulling over the Cape Horn ads displayed on her tack board.

She paused at the edge of her desk. "Logan, you can't be worried about the Matthews Agency."

Her question was met with silence. Just when she thought he hadn't heard her, he absently glanced in her direction. "Hmm? No, not really," he said, shaking his head, but she could hear the hollowness in his tone.

"She's going to lose the account, you have to know that. Virginia Matthews only knows how to sell one thing and that's sex. Marc is looking for something different. We know that."

Logan picked up one of their proposed magazine ads and studied the couple strolling along the white sand. "You're sure we haven't played this too conservatively?"

"Yes, I am," she said without an ounce of uncertainty. "We've gone over this, Logan." She stepped to her credenza, pulled the folder of the Matthews Agency's current Cape Horn campaign and began thumbing through the ads. "Marc's daughter recently turned eleven. She's starting to blossom into a young woman. That's a point in a father's life when he starts seeing things differently. It's often frightening to men, to see their baby dressing like a woman, wearing bras, developing curves."

She pulled several of Virginia's ads from the file, crossed the office and held one in front of Logan. It was a picture of two lovers on the beach, the woman practically naked and the man resting intently on top of her. "Look at this ad. This model can't be more than fifteen years old. I guarantee you, every time Marc looks at this ad, he places his daughter's face on this girl."

"How do you know that?"

"My cousin has a ten-year-old. He fumed when I showed him this ad. He felt it promoted teen sex and

I have to agree. There's nothing mature about this couple." She flipped through the rest of the ads. "They're all the same, Logan. They're practically children on the brink of having sex. This isn't Marc Tyndale, especially since the death of his first wife. I know what he's thinking. He feels a responsibility to his daughter's mother, to make sure he does right by their child. I know he's grown uncomfortable with these ads. He's all but said so in the meetings."

Logan studied the ads in front of him, but Trisha didn't see any sign of relief in his eyes. He was still worried.

"Logan, Marc Tyndale just remarried. You know about his new wife. Corinne Beauchamp's family is very wealthy, very influential and devoutly Catholic. Senator Beauchamp is a staunch conservative Republican. Marc's got to be thinking how these ads might appear to his new in-laws."

"Virginia knows all this."

"But she doesn't know how to run a tasteful ad campaign." Trisha crossed to her desk, opened a second folder and began spreading ads across the desktop. "Look at these. Perfume, running shoes, fitness spas," she said as Logan stepped to the desk. "They're all the same, half-naked women, all barely of legal age. Virginia doesn't know how to advertise in any other way."

She held out another ad. "Look at this one. It's milk, for heaven's sake. By the look of this ad, you'd assume she was selling breast milk."

The comment finally prompted a warm chuckle from Logan that brought flutters to her stomach.

She lowered her tone. "She's going to overplay her

hand. Marc may have told her he wants something more reserved, but she's working to her own scale. She may pull it back, but she'll still cross the line. I promise you. She hasn't got an agent on her staff who knows how to pull it back, and even if someone did, she'd outrank them and turn up the heat."

She stepped to his side and placed a hand on his arm. "We need to stick to our plan. She's going to shoot herself in the foot, I promise you."

Logan turned and met her gaze, prompting that familiar heat to simmer in her veins. The fear and concern in his eyes had drained away, replaced by a resolute sense of assuredness and a soft smile of appreciation warmed his face.

The fact that she'd been able to calm him filled her heart with need. So many times she'd seen torment in his eyes that left her aching to make it go away. And the fact that she'd just proved she could doubled her desire to dig deeper until she unearthed his turmoil and truly knew the man underneath.

Logan's gaze deepened, his eyes stayed fixed on hers, heating the air and the space around her. She wanted to look away. She needed to look away, but her eyes held on those beautiful, dark pools. Every muscle in her body seemed to cement in place, unable to move, and she quickly became entranced by the fire in his gaze.

Her hand dropped from his arm, but her eyes ignored her urgent pleas to glance away. Her breath caught short, her heart began a firm, steady beat that rose to thunder when he lifted a hand and lightly caressed it down her arm.

The touch sparked a sizzle on her skin that traveled through her veins and sped down to her toes, and somewhere in all the desire, she heard herself whisper, "Trust me."

His eyes darkened with need. His smile faded, replaced by something sensual and seductive. He lifted his hand and gently pressed her chin between his thumb and forefinger, holding it there, burning her cheeks with fire.

The room grew flaming hot. Seconds seemed like hours as he held his eyes on hers, then slowly moved his gaze to her mouth.

His lips twitched. He cocked his head to the side and bent his chin forward the slightest inch and she realized he was going to kiss her.

His eyes held her lips as if he were studying them, musing over how they might feel pressed against his mouth and the deep look of intent in his gaze snatched her breath completely. No part of her body could move other than the fierce pounding of her heart as she waited for what would surely come next.

His hand swept from her chin and lightly caressed over her cheek, just a brush of a finger that tensed every nerve in her body. Her breasts went tight and a clench jolted between her thighs. His fresh, spring scent surrounded her making her dizzy with want, but her eyes wouldn't close, her lids couldn't blink. She was stuck on his gaze and the swelling need that rose with every thump of her heart.

His chin dipped lower, the movement barely noticeable to the naked eye, but she could see it through the focus of his stare. He was inching toward her, his eyes growing more intense, until gently, cautiously, he pressed his lips to hers.

A blizzard of sparks rushed through her body, pricking her skin and sending her heart into an all-out race. Logan was actually kissing her, his warm hand cupping her cheek, his fingers caressing the back of her neck.

Shock numbed her thoughts of everything but the touch of those lips against hers—real lips, not imaginary, cyberlips that existed only in her thoughts. These lips hummed her senses and as she opened her mouth in welcome, she inhaled a deep breath, wanting to soak in his essence, absorb the feel of his hard chest pressed against hers and relish in the firm beat of his heart.

A weary groan crept from his throat as his caution dissolved and he drove the kiss deeper. It was a groan filled with need, laced with agony she fully understood. Months of want, years of restraint and denial building over time, the groan marked a final point of tired surrender.

His hand trailed around her waist, pulling her against his chest, and Trisha sank into the embrace, allowing his touch to soothe and comfort like a soft, down bed. His grasp was firm, but kind, the kiss greedy, yet tender, just as she always knew it would be, and as his strong arms caressed her, she realized this kiss would never be enough.

Their tongues danced, their hands explored, and the moans that escaped them both spoke of deep, driving need. But just as the fog started lifting, just as reality crept in, Logan stiffened in her arms and quickly jerked away.

7

LOGAN TOOK TWO shaky steps back, ran a hand through his hair then brushed it over his face as his mind tried to comprehend what the hell he'd just done.

"Damn, Trisha, I don't know what came over me." He took another step toward the door. "I'm sorry. That was completely inappropriate."

Trisha was clearly stunned, but still managed a few words of assurance. "Logan, it's okay."

He shook his head, intent on disagreeing. "No, it's not okay. That was inappropriate and I apologize. It won't happen again. Please, believe that."

"Logan, really, I understand and it's okay."

He swiped his hand against the back of his neck, keeping his eyes planted firmly on the floor. Trisha's voice was calm, but he didn't dare look to see if her ease was sincere. He was too ashamed to make eye contact and too fearful of what he might do if he surrendered to those sparkling blues again.

"It's just…" he stuttered, trying to recapture his senses. "It's just Virginia. She has a way of getting to me. But my actions were inexcusable. It won't happen again."

He stepped to the edge of the door, the need to get

out of Trisha's office overwhelming any other thought in his mind. "I'm sorry," he said again. "I'll let you get back to work."

He left her office, his long strides carrying him away quickly.

What the hell had he done? What could have possessed him to pop off and kiss Trisha Bain? He wanted to blink and wake up, to discover it was all a bad dream, but the scent of her perfume lingered as proof that it had really happened.

And wasn't that just brilliant?

Crossing his office, he dropped into his chair and groaned a flustered sigh. That had to have been the stupidest move he could have made. So Virginia had given him doubts about the campaign. He should have shrugged them off instead of wandering into the office of the one woman who'd tempted him since the divorce.

He'd been vulnerable, he'd needed reassurance. Did it occur to him that Trisha would have responded with exactly the words he'd needed to hear? Or that those intelligent, soothing words would have pushed him to kiss her?

Angry and bewildered, he rose from his chair and stepped to the window. The glow of the lights from the building across the street, the soft twinkle of the water on the bay, the busy span of the Bay bridge, all brought back thoughts of his last chat with Scorpio63. He'd wanted her in his life—for real, where he could taste and touch her and a side of him wondered if it was his yearning for Scorpio that had turned his eyes to Trisha. When she'd taken his arm and spoken so genuinely, assuring him that things would work out the way he'd wanted, a side of him felt as if he was talking to Scorpio.

Could this cyberfantasy be twisting his head?

He let out the breath he'd been holding and for the first time wondered whether he should be engaging in online sex. Maybe living in a fantasy was just confusing his real life, leaving him so empty with need he was willing to reach out and grab the nearest woman he could find.

But then he remembered how bad his life had been before Scorpio and immediately reversed his opinion.

She was helping, even with this recent lapse. She'd become his escape, his avenue to forget a stressful day and sink into the warmth and comfort of someone who wanted nothing more from him than his attention and loving arms.

Even if they were just cyberarms.

So maybe he had confused her with Trisha in a subconscious way. He'd just have to work harder to keep things straight in his head, because the last thing he needed was to give Trisha a false impression. Yes, she was bright and attractive, but that wasn't enough for him to break the promises he'd made to himself. Mixing business and romance didn't work. And until he found the right woman for his life, he'd need to work harder to keep the two in check.

"I'VE BEEN WAITING for our time together, more than any other day."

"I've been waiting, too," Trisha typed then clicked Send.

"I've done a lot of thinking lately. About our relationship."

Trisha perked as she read Pisces47's words on the screen. She'd heard words like that before. They were always the start of a Dear Jane speech, usually followed by, "It's me, not you." In most other situations, she'd feel that wash of dread, but tonight Logan's words filled her with hope.

The moment he'd kissed her in her office she'd decided to end her relationship with Pisces. It had been the moment she'd waited for, the one clear sign that she had a solid chance with Logan.

And for sure, it didn't get much clearer than a hot, passionate kiss.

Now that she knew, she needed to put this cyberfling behind them so she could start focusing on what she really wanted from her life and her career. She still wasn't sure she wanted the VP job—if it would even be offered—but she definitely wanted to explore a relationship with Logan and she couldn't do that while deceiving him about Scorpio.

Her plan was to simply make an excuse, explain that she'd become involved with another man and that this cybersex wasn't right, put Pisces behind her so she could begin to pursue Logan with nothing but honesty. Maybe in the future she'd tell him about Scorpio if things worked out between them. But for now, she needed to make this break to clear the confusion and start off on the right foot.

She'd been nervous, afraid this moment would crush his heart or hurt his feelings, but his comment gave her hope. Could he be breaking this off? It was a dream too good to be true. If she were to paint the ideal picture of how this ended, they would part on mutual terms, both wanting to end the affair, leaving neither of them wounded.

Her fingers raced to coax him along. "I've been doing a lot of thinking, too. Please, tell me what you've been thinking about."

She crossed her fingers and toes.

"You fulfill a need, in more ways than I'd ever imagined you could. And it wasn't until today that I realized how important you are to me. Like this. In our cyberworld. Two souls joining without the interference of the outside world."

She uncrossed her fingers and toes as her heart dropped in her chest.

"What do you mean?" she typed.

"I'm sorry, honey. I know this wasn't what you expected. I just...before we started tonight, I wanted to let you know that you mean more to me than sex. You do more for me than just fulfill a physical need. And until today, I never really understood how important this time is to me. How much you do for me."

This can't be happening.

She stared at the screen, suddenly losing all notion of how she was going to deal with this.

"I'm glad I've been good for you," she typed, feeling the need to do something other than leave his words hanging on the screen.

Logan was right. She hadn't expected this. It was the giant curve ball that swung around and cocked her in the back of her head.

He needed her. And he chose to admit that on the day she finally got the courage to break it off.

Courage.

The word repeated in her mind.

As cruel as it seemed at the moment, she had no choice. She had to break this off. And with that thought, she raised her hands to the keyboard.

"Pisces, I'd like to talk," she typed, trying to quickly recall the speech she had practiced in her head. Why she hadn't written it down was beyond her. At the moment, she could really use those words, because they seemed to have completely escaped her brain.

"Come to bed with me, honey. I'll put my arms around you and we can talk, if you'd like."

He wanted her in bed? They'd never had cybersex in bed. She wasn't sure why, but for whatever reason, they hadn't and the notion struck her as odd.

"Okay," she typed, trying to clear her confusion and get back her goal.

"You look so beautiful tonight. I can't take my eyes off you and my heart aches to remove these clothes, so we can lay together, with no barriers between us."

"Okay," she typed again, cursing the word the moment it appeared on the screen. She needed to stop this chat.

"Climb under the covers with me. I want to feel your silky skin against me. I want to wrap my legs around yours and cradle you in my arms."

His words lit a fire that ached in her belly. How she wished they were really together in bed. She didn't want the cyber Logan anymore. Not now that she'd had a taste of the real thing. She wanted him in the flesh, to really feel the hardness of his chest, to lace her fingers through his hair and feel the warmth of his body as he whispered those sweet words in her ear.

"You feel so good against me. It's cold outside and your body brings warmth that I feel from my skin all the way to my heart. I pull you close and press my lips to your forehead as I soak in the sweet scent of your hair."

She couldn't help but close her eyes for a moment and imagine the scene, imagine the words coming from Logan's lips when he'd kissed her in his office, and when she did, her throat began to tighten. This had to end, and she wondered what kind of curse had been set upon her to make this so hard.

"I run my hand down your smooth back and grab a handful of your soft behind. Just the feel of you in my arms makes me hard with desire and my chest swell with need."

Her mouth ran dry. She swallowed. Why tonight's, of all chats, did he choose to express such tender affection?

"I sink my face into the curve of your neck and pull your body closer. I want to drink you in. Your essence is intoxicating and I kiss at your neck, your shoulder, wanting to take in more."

His words continued to roll over the screen as she felt her frustration build. Logan was hot tonight, but in his words, she saw a level of endearment she'd never seen before. As she continued scanning the text, thoughts of this afternoon mixed with the words in front of her, were spinning her in confusion. The feel of Logan's hand this afternoon, cupped against her cheek, entwined with her image of his body against hers. She dreamed of those lips she'd kissed today, pressing along her bare shoulder and she wanted them here for real. She took a breath and inhaled his masculine scent that still clung to her blouse; she wanted that scent everywhere.

His words of seduction continued to flood her mind and her heart began a furious race. Allowing him to go on wasn't right. She had to break this off now, and she fought the heat he brought to her skin. Her body still wanted to cling to the words on the screen, but her mind needed to make them stop.

"Please," she typed, trying to end the torment, but Logan wasn't listening. He just kept tempting her sexual desire, dragging the climax out, and the more he went on, the more anxious she became.

"I'm holding you on the edge, honey, trying to keep you on the brink of ecstasy. I want to relish every morsel of your body, quivering against mine. You're begging me, urging me to move faster."

Faster, yes. She needed this over. She needed to end the whirlwind that muddled her thoughts. Her fingers stiffened, her pulse sped. Thoughts of their kiss continued to spin through her mind. Oh, God, she couldn't think, couldn't think.

"Beg for it, honey. Beg me to take you."

"Please," she typed. "Please," she spoke. She didn't want to read the words on the screen. She wanted to hear them, have them whispered in her ear while the weight of his body pressed against her chest.

"Beg me, honey. Beg me."

"Logan, please." She typed her reply, her thoughts spinning in circles.

Moments passed, her hands went numb from fisting as she waited for Logan to provide the final release that would allow her to collect her thoughts and move on.

But the words didn't come.

The screen fell silent.

Too silent.

She glanced at the last passage as the jolt of fear ripped through her chest.

Logan.

She'd called him Logan.

Her mind buzzed and kept her from focusing on anything other than the stillness of the screen. Her breath stopped short and a blizzard of trembles started at the base of her spine and spread throughout her body.

Her eyes darted to a blip on the screen.

"Who is this?"

She didn't want to answer and the idea raced to the front of her brain. She could shut off the computer, cancel her account and never log on again.

But despite the dizzying ache in her head, she knew it wasn't an option. LoveSigns.com had her name. Logan didn't know who she was, but the service did, and she wondered if Logan could find a way to have her name released. It was highly doubtful, but could she afford that chance?

Nausea swept through her as she tried to think clearly. Maybe if she could walk away and take some time to consider how to handle the situation. Then she'd be prepared to explain herself and the reasons behind her actions.

Her heart thundered against her rib cage. Short breaths escaped her lungs as she tried to get more air.

The words repeated on the screen.

"Who is this?"

Fright widened her eyes. She backed away from the computer as if it held lethal poison. Her thoughts quickly sped to Logan and humiliation sickened her. Humiliation for both of them.

What would he think?

What would he do?

She had to do something. Making him wait for an answer would just infuriate him, drag out the agony and make this worse.

She had no choice, and her heart dropped as she conceded her only option.

With shaking fingers, she entered the word, "Trisha" and clicked Send.

Instantly more words followed.

"Trisha who?"

Tears welled in her eyes as she added, "Trisha Bain", then waited for the ax to fall.

But nothing came.

Only the message that Pisces47 had signed off.

As darkness settled over her bedroom, she stared at the words, hoping somehow they'd transform into proof that what just happened was nothing more than a nightmare. That she'd dreamed it all, that it had been her imagination playing tricks on her thanks to the stress of the last few days.

But the words never changed.

It had really happened.

Logan Moore knew she was the woman he'd been chatting with. He knew she'd been aware of his identity and had chosen to keep it to herself. She'd lied to him. Betrayed his trust. And she wasn't sure if she was more devastated over the thought of losing her job or losing Logan for good.

What was he doing?

What was he thinking?

Pain stabbed her heart as she considered everything that could be going through his mind. She'd come so close. She'd been so near to taking a piece of Logan, she could taste it and now it was gone.

She held her hands in front of her and watched as her hopes for a future with Logan drained like sand between her fingers. And given that she'd lied to him, she doubted her future with the agency, too.

But oddly, the loss of her job didn't seem to be the source of her pain, and it was a revelation she hadn't expected. She knew she'd recover her career, but any hope of a future with Logan was completely severed, and that reality brought an ache to her heart and anguish to her gut.

Up until now, she hadn't realized how much she'd wanted him. She'd told herself she would find another job and move on, but now she realized, that was never a viable option. She'd been enamored with Logan Moore, so infatuated that she knew she would have stuck around for years, as long as there was a shred of hope the two of them might have had a chance together.

So maybe in that regard, this was all meant to be. Maybe fate had stepped in and forced the decision she herself would never have made.

It was surely made now.

8

Daily Love Horoscope for Pisces

Looking for that someone special? Have you checked what's under your nose? Not your lips, silly, but they may come in handy very soon. Pay attention to those around you. You may find your perfect mate has been there all along.

LOGAN STARED at the screen in utter disbelief, reading the words over and over until his brain conceded that what he was seeing was the truth.

Trisha Bain.

Scorpio63 was Trisha Bain.

It was too incredible to believe. And too outstanding to chalk up to coincidence. Ice rushed through his veins as anger swept over him. This couldn't be a coincidence. There was just no way.

His mind flashed back to his brother, Dane, handing him the brochure and the note with the Web address, user name and password. Dane had hooked him up with LoveSigns, sending Logan straight into the arms of Trisha Bain. But it didn't add up.

Dane didn't know Trisha. Logan was certain the two had never even met. And besides, Dane wouldn't have gone behind his back to pull something like this. It wasn't Dane's style.

But Dane had handed him the brochure at the office. Could Trisha have overheard their conversation?

Someone had to be behind this. No other answer made sense.

He pressed his palms to his face. The question of "How" spun so feverishly through his mind, he couldn't stop to sort out anything else. Those chats. All the things he'd said. All the things he'd virtually done. The thought rushed a wave of mortifying heat through him.

Every day, he'd worked with her, going through the motions like casual business partners, all the while holding his desire for her body with tight-fisted reins.

And in the end, he'd been going home and unwittingly screwing her senseless.

The irony alone could make his head explode.

But why would Trisha have done this? What could she possibly have to gain? Clearly, she'd used Love-Signs to get to him somehow. But even that didn't sit right. Pisces and Scorpio had never spoken about business. They'd rarely even shared specific details of their lives. For months, the two had done nothing more than comfort one another. They'd simply played out sexual fantasies and provided each other a release from the pressures of the day. She'd never asked for anything more, or questioned him about his business or his life. If this had been a ploy to gain something, Logan couldn't fathom what it was.

Which left his notion of a conspiracy seeming more and more unlikely.

Once again the question of "How?" spun through his mind. How did he end up paired with Trisha, and if it was by sheer accident, how could she have known it was him?

The questions churned through his brain until his thoughts grew numb and comprehension completely abandoned him. He had no idea what he should be thinking, and even less, how he should feel.

Scorpio was Trisha Bain.

God, what was he supposed to do with that?

So many times, he'd wanted to know who Scorpio really was, but fear had kept him from going there. His rational mind had formed a probable image of Scorpio in the flesh, and his cynicism about Internet relationships had prevented him from suggesting they trade photos or details about their lives no matter how badly he'd been tempted at times. He hadn't wanted to ruin the fantasy woman he'd created in his head.

But now he knew who she was and the repercussions exceeded any fear he could have concocted.

He flashed to their kiss in her office and his thoughts whipped into a flurry of embarrassment, anger and confusion. She'd known he was Pisces when he'd kissed her and her response to the kiss was definitely pleasure. Yet she'd stood there and brushed it off as if it were no big deal.

What had she been thinking?

He pushed away from the computer. He had too many questions, not a single answer and a headache raging between his temples. Stiff and shaken, he made his way to the kitchen, popped two aspirin then grabbed his keys.

It was time to get answers.

TRISHA STEPPED from the shower, grabbed a towel and dried off. She'd hoped the hot, steaming water would have lifted her spirits, eased her mind and allowed her to see things more clearly.

It accomplished none of those. Her body still felt like lead, weighted by her loss.

How could a day have started out so stunning and ended up in such a mess? She'd give anything to step back two weeks and do it all over. She would have done so many things differently.

She crossed her bedroom and slipped on a pair of pajama bottoms and a light, sleeveless tee. She needed to formulate how she would handle Logan tomorrow morning. She owed him an explanation, but as she rehearsed the words in her mind, everything she came up with sounded wrong. One side wanted to draft her resignation and simply slip out the door, but she owed him more than that, not just as Logan, her employer, but as Pisces47, her former lover.

Stepping from her bedroom, a sharp rap on the door brought her to a halt.

"Trisha? It's Logan."

Her feet rooted in place as she stared at the door. Of all the scenarios that had played through her head, Logan showing up at her apartment hadn't been one of them. She wasn't prepared for this. She needed more time, and as she tried to pull her thoughts together, she heard the quick knock once again.

"Trisha."

The intent in his tone swept her feet into action, and with shaky hands, she turned the lock and opened the door.

One look at Logan's dark, midnight eyes sent a crackling awareness snapping through her. She'd guessed he'd never look at her the same way again and now she knew for sure. The intensity of his stare, the knowing look in his eyes, left her feeling naked.

A shower of tears threatened to humiliate her further, but she willed them back. She'd had enough embarrassment for one day. Instead, she swallowed hard and forced herself to meet his gaze.

"I need answers," he said, his voice low and stern.

Unable to speak, she simply backed away from the door, leaving him room to enter. His eyes dropped to her chest and she glanced down to see hardened nipples piercing her light cotton tee. Her cheeks flushed with heat. She crossed her arms at her waist as Logan passed through the threshold and closed the door behind him.

"Let me just throw on a sweater," she said as she darted into her bedroom.

LOGAN TOOK A BREATH and glanced around the apartment as he waited for Trisha to return. Though he'd dropped her off here once, he hadn't come inside, and as his eyes trailed around the room, he realized it was exactly what he would have expected. The plush cushy couch was tasteful yet comfortable, draped with soft pillows and a caramel-colored chenille throw. The bur-gundy wing chairs spoke of elegance, but their casual striped uphol-stery kept the feel inviting. Original artwork mixed with scented candles, soft lighting brought warmth.

In short, it had Scorpio written all over it and as if he hadn't truly believed it before, the thought that Trisha was Scorpio63 finally set in.

His eyes met hers when she stepped back into the room. Those breasts that had just taunted him were now covered with a thick U.C. Berkeley sweatshirt, which was a good thing. He'd come here to get answers, not end up in another embrace and the last thing he needed was Trisha half-exposed, making this even more uncomfortable.

She stood near the entrance to the hall, still clutch-ing her arms around her waist. She seemed so nervous, so vulnerable, that he felt like an intruder intent on do-ing harm. It tugged at his heart. He hadn't come here to intimidate her, he just wanted answers, and given the tortured look on her face, he decided the quicker he got them, the quicker he could end her torment and go home.

He opened his mouth to ask, but she spoke first.

"Can I offer you a drink?"

Logan shook his head. "No, thanks." He took a breath to regroup. "What I want is an explanation."

He saw the muscles in her neck contort as she swal-lowed hard and then moved to one of the chairs. She sat on the edge of the cushion, her hands folded tightly in her lap.

"I didn't know you were Pisces. Not before Thursday."

"You're telling me this is just a coincidence?"

Her blue eyes widened with shock. She clearly hadn't expected that response, which meant she was either sincere or very, very good.

"What? You think I arranged this?" She stopped speaking, but her mouth didn't close.

"What else am I supposed to think? This could hardly be coincidence. And this afternoon, in your office…" He couldn't utter the word kiss so he skipped it and simply shook his head. "How could you just stand there and not say anything?"

She gasped. "What was I supposed to say? 'Hey, you're better in person than you are online'? I'm having just as much trouble with this as you are."

Frustration closed in on him. "I don't understand how this happened. What were you doing on a Web site like that?"

He hadn't meant for the comment to sound so possessive, but that was the way it came out, like a father who'd just caught his teenage daughter having sex in the back of his Chevy.

Her mouth dropped wider. Flames lit in her eyes. This was not going well. The tables were turning and he quickly needed to turn them back. It was Trisha who had the explaining to do.

"How could I have arranged this?" she finally asked.

"Then how do you explain it?"

The question stopped her in her tracks. She blinked, pausing to formulate an answer, providing Logan with a badly needed break. His heart was pounding, his headache was creeping back and the last thing he'd expected was her angry glare.

"I don't know," she said. "I assume something in our profiles put us together."

"What profile?"

"The questionnaire you filled out when you signed up for the service." She sat back in the chair and exhaled a deep huff. "We both have a lot in common, you know. Our careers, where we live, our ages aren't far apart. They could have used any of those similarities to match us together."

"I thought this was some astrology thing."

"Yes, but the questions on the form carried weight, too."

Realization drained the tension in his shoulders, causing them to drop. "I never filled out a form," he admitted. "My brother signed me up. All I got was a password and a date. I didn't even know there was a questionnaire."

"Logan," she said, the anger in her voice subsiding, "I didn't know Pisces was you before last week. I swear."

He studied the look in her eyes and saw nothing but staunch sincerity. Slowly he shook his head. "I don't understand. If this is all legit, then how did you know who I was?"

"I heard you on the phone. You said, 'Whenever you need me, I'm just a click away,' just like Pisces. That was the first time I had any idea you two might be the same."

His mind swept back to last Thursday, the scenes flashing through his mind like pictures in a slideshow. Trisha standing in his office, the ad campaign scattered on the floor, the fright he'd seen in her eyes and that lame excuse she'd given for her actions. It was all un-folding in front of him, and the more he reflected on that day, the more shaken he became.

He moved to the couch and took a seat. "I think I'll take that drink now."

Trisha jumped up from the chair and stepped to the kitchen, returning moments later with a glass of Scotch. He shot it down in one gulp.

More memories seeped through the fog. "The chat last week," he said. "You had me describe my office."

She refilled his glass and left the bottle on the maple coffee table. "I'm sorry," she said, returning to her seat. Her voice had lowered to that comforting tone that al-ways eased his nerves like a hot, steamy spa. "I didn't know how else to find out. I mean, it's not something you just come out and ask."

"No, I guess not." He took his time with the second shot, taking small sips to allow the heat to simmer down his throat. The transcript of the chat played back through his mind, bringing clarity to everything Trisha had said.

He huffed in a bitter laugh. "Wild bronze horses," he muttered.

Her voice was barely a whisper. "I'm sorry. I had to find a way to be sure."

Oh, God, he thought. Was this really just some twist of fate? His skeptical side didn't want to believe it, but he knew the odds of Trisha intentionally putting them together were miniscule, especially without help from Dane. And though he had trouble trusting Trisha, he un-doubtedly trusted Dane.

The situation was incredible, but he couldn't doubt what Trisha was saying. It all fit.

A quick huff swept out his nose as he crooked his mouth and shook his head. Brilliant. Absolutely brilliant. For the past three months, he'd been fucking his marketing director over the Internet. If it wasn't so humiliating, he'd be rolling on the floor with laughter.

"I tried to break it off."

He looked up to meet her gaze. "You what?"

"Tonight, I tried to break it off. I just…I got flustered. I was going to make an excuse to end it."

"And keep it to yourself?"

She nodded.

He set the glass on the table and ran a hand through his hair. This was all so much to absorb in such a short time, he wasn't sure how to react or feel. Would it have been better if he'd never known? Probably. Though he didn't like the idea of Trisha keeping the secret.

Then again, knowing wasn't so hot, either.

His eyes shot to Trisha. "Who else knows about this?"

Her caged expression told him someone did, and it wasn't hard to guess who.

"Oh, shit, Trisha," he said with a sigh.

"Adrienne swore she hasn't told Bill."

"Great," he muttered, reaching a hand up to clasp the back of his neck.

"I believe her. I don't think Bill knows."

He couldn't help the sour chuckle. "Oh, I know he doesn't. Bill wouldn't be able to keep a whopper like this."

"She'll keep it to herself if I ask her."

"Please do."

He took a long, deep breath, picked up his glass and downed the last of his Scotch. So much for nursing it. But then again, if there was ever a time to get drunk, this would be it.

"Look," Trisha said, stirring him from his thoughts. "Devon is very capable of handling the Tyndale account, if we should get it."

Her comment hit him like a slap to the head. He glanced up and met her eyes. "You talk as if you're going somewhere."

Her expression was pained. Her mouth bobbed for a moment before she replied, "I just assumed...under the circumstances."

"You're quitting?" Panic sped through his chest. This was the last thing he'd expected and the last thing he wanted. Despite the humiliation, he wasn't ready to lose the best marketing director he had.

"I...no. I just assumed."

"I have no intention of firing you, if that's what you're thinking."

He held his eyes on hers. Though the tension remained, he made out a twinkle of relief.

"Look, Trisha. Obviously, neither of us asked for this. This is just...I don't know what it is, but I certainly don't want you to leave the company. You're important to me."

Her startled gaze darkened. "For Tyndale," she said.

"Yes, for Tyndale and every other account I expect you'll land after him." Jitters in his stomach caused him to rise and pace the floor. So much had happened in the last hour. He'd gone from suspicion and anger to understanding and relief and simmering under it was a big pool of shame. He was as embarrassed as Trisha, but never in the mix of it all did he think she'd resign.

And never in the mix of it all did he think he'd want her to stay. But he did. Set aside the embarrassment, he'd just found Scorpio and though none of this had really begun to sink in, a tiny side of his gut felt a twinge of excitement.

Trisha remained silent, her eyes focused squarely in her lap, her face riddled with the same confusion he felt.

"Trisha," he said, calming his voice intentionally. "We've…inadvertently had an affair. It's awkward, I agree. But if you can move beyond it, I certainly can."

Her eyes moved to meet his gaze, and the sense of hope he saw in them fed his own ease. He didn't want to think of losing her and if he was reading her correctly, he wasn't going to have to.

"Yes, of course, I can."

He exhaled the breath in his lungs. Okay, one problem down. How many more to go?

An uncomfortable silence fell over the room, leaving Logan to wonder what should come next. Technically, he had the explanation he'd come for, but turning and walking away didn't seem right. At the same time, staying much longer didn't seem wise, either. Though he'd received his answers, processing them would take a bit longer.

From the moment he'd stepped in this room, he'd been shooting from the hip, reacting on instinct, not having the opportunity to truly absorb and calculate his actions or how he should feel.

All he knew was, he didn't want to give up Trisha, and for what reasons, he still wasn't exactly sure.

"So," he said. "We move on. We go back to business and put this behind us."

She nodded, her face displaying the same exhaustion that was beginning to overwhelm him.

"This is an awkward situation," he added. "But I'm sure, after a few days, we'll find a way to deal with it."

She managed a faint smile that helped him buy his own words.

"Okay," he said, moving to the door.

Trisha rose to see him out, opening the door and allowing him to pass. He hesitated at the threshold, his body begging him to do something more than just nod and walk out.

Turning to face her, he took a moment to drink in her gaze. This *was* Scorpio, his tender, sacred Scorpio. Of all the women he'd imagined, none of them matched Trisha's beauty and his heart ached to reach out and touch her, to caress his hand over that shiny brown hair, to press his lips to hers.

He reached down and took her hand in his, causing a flush of pink to swarm over her cheeks. It was the same faint hue he'd seen after he'd kissed her in her office and the memory fed his urge to kiss her again. He wanted to feel those soft lips against his again, stoke a fire in his belly and bring life to the body he'd once thought dead.

Scorpio was Trisha Bain. It still didn't seem real, and he had to blink to believe it. The woman who had taunted his body by day was the same woman who had stolen his heart at night. Put the two together and he had a package only an idiot would refuse.

Idiot.

The word stuck in his mind and he quickly released his grasp. Had he learned nothing from Virginia? Scorpio or not, Trisha was his employee. Was he that stupid that he would just waltz down the same path that nearly destroyed him once before?

Apparently.

But a voice inside reminded him that not every woman was Virginia. Scorpio wasn't. He would have banked his estate on that. But could he really be sure?

That was the question of the day.

Trisha kept staring into his eyes, the gray flecks in those crystal blues sparkling against the dim porch light. He wanted to move closer and study each fleck until he could draw them in his mind.

Standing here, with the cool coastal breeze flushing her cheeks, Logan realized how beautiful Trisha really was and the revelation brought new torment to his already flustered state. His body begged him to kiss her, his memory fought for control, humiliation urged him to turn and run and in the mix of it all he felt all he could do was to wait it out to see which emotion won.

"What are you thinking?" Trisha whispered.

Her quiet voice broke the silence and shook him from his thoughts.

"That I should go home."

Trisha nodded and took a step back. "Then I'll see you in the morning," she said.

He blinked, then blinked again.

"Yes. I'll see you in the morning."

TRISHA CLOSED THE DOOR, pressed her back to the wall and slowly slid to the floor. Her thoughts muddled, her body shaken, she stared at the room, trying to make sense of what had just happened.

She hadn't lost her job. She hadn't lost Logan. And for a moment, she nearly had to pinch herself to believe it was really true. Never in her wildest dreams did she believe he'd forgive her so quickly and be willing to move on. Not after what she had done.

But once again, Logan surprised her by his unyielding faith. He'd believed her. Without the slightest indignation, he'd understood her motives and held none of her actions against her. Even she had underestimated him and the thought brought an ache to her heart. If she'd ever wanted Logan before, her desire doubled tonight.

She pulled herself from the floor, crossed to her bedroom and dropped back on her bed. Staring at the ceiling, she wondered what she should do next. This was shaky ground. Surely, Logan would be studying her over the next few weeks, examining whether or not they would be able to restore their business relationship after what had transpired. He'd be hesitant, wondering if their online tryst would affect her performance on the job.

It wouldn't. She would make sure of that. Surely, if Logan was reluctant to get involved, one of the reasons would be his fear of ruining their business relationship. Her next steps would ease that fear. She would show him that she could stay professional no matter what happened in their personal lives, that a love affair wouldn't affect her performance on the job.

She'd back off. Let things wind down. Demonstrate that despite their past as lovers, she could stay focused. And once she convinced him of that, it would be one more strike in her favor.

After that, she had no idea.

She wondered how he must be taking this. He'd been able to look at her. The situation hadn't sickened him to the point where he couldn't work with her again. That must be a good sign. The man had kissed her, after all, and if she wasn't mistaken, he'd nearly kissed her again just now.

But he hadn't shown up smiling, either. It obviously hadn't thrilled him to discover she was Scorpio. He hadn't wrapped her in his arms and thanked the gods he'd found her. Could LoveSigns really have just been about sex? Had Scorpio been nothing more to him than a physical release?

She shook her head. Pisces and Scorpio had been more than sex. She had to believe that. Logan was simply reacting while in a state of shock. Honestly, no matter what he'd done tonight, she couldn't rely on any of it. He'd been stunned. He'd needed answers. The reality of this situation would take more time to comprehend. Which was all the more reason she needed to play it cool for a while. She'd show him he didn't have to fear losing her professionally. She could be his lover and work in his office.

And that's exactly what she would do.

9

LOGAN POPPED THE CORK on the champagne bottle, prompting a round of applause from his staff, although he didn't feel like celebrating. In the week since finding out about Scorpio, Trisha had acted as if nothing had happened between them. It was as if she'd waved a wand and the affair between Pisces and Scorpio never existed. She was her normal, bright self, calm, casual and strictly business. Not once had she brought up the affair, or given him any sign that Pisces had mattered to her in the slightest and he couldn't help the feeling of déjà vu.

Virginia had done the very same thing. After years of deep affection, sharing his bed, his hopes, his fears, Virginia had one day flicked the switch when she casually dropped her bomb. Their years together hadn't meant a thing. She mentioned enjoying the sex, appreciating the car maintenance and the month-long vacations, but that was about it. Everything else had been part of the job, her way of climbing the corporate ladder.

From that point on their relationship had become a professional war and his heart, his dreams and his future were nothing more than collateral damage. Virginia had skipped off without a wince of regret, giving him the same calm brush-off he was receiving from Trisha Bain right now.

He tipped the bottle and began filling glasses. He supposed he should be grateful. He hadn't wanted the affair with Trisha to ruin their working relationship and it certainly hadn't. Everything between them was business as usual, and as her employer, he was thankful. But as her former lover, it shot a stake through his heart. He was now standing here, staring at the woman with whom he'd shared his darkest secrets. She knew things about him he hadn't told a soul, and as Scorpio, she'd been warm and receptive, as if she'd understood his needs and shared his hopes and desires.

But Trisha Bain wasn't batting an eyelash. The woman he'd worked so hard to keep from wanting by day had just brushed the relationship off as if their private evening chats hadn't meant a thing, and once again, he'd found himself on the wrong side of a one-sided love affair.

Trisha obviously hadn't missed Pisces, and though he mourned the loss of his lover, he celebrated the fact that at least this time, his business was still intact.

Emptying the bottle into the final flute, he raised a glass and forced a pleasant smile. A scatter of clinking glasses brought everyone's attention to the front of the large conference room.

When the crowd grew silent, he gave a toast. "To Tyndale and our new vice president of travel."

The crowd cheered and whistled. The smile on

Trisha's face lit the room, sending another chill shivering through his body. He'd had a celebration very much like this when he'd announced Virginia as a full partner and Virginia's smile had beamed just as brightly. But he reminded himself that Virginia never had Trisha's talent, and no matter what had happened between Pisces and Scorpio, Trisha's promotion was genuinely deserved.

She met his gaze and accepted the toast, her face displaying nothing more than professional sincerity. She didn't hold the glance for that extra beat. There was no flicker of fire in her eyes. There was nothing that went beyond simple appreciation and the moment she took a sip of her drink, she darted her eyes away.

Once again, his chest filled with bitter disappointment that he worked hard to shrug off. It was silly, really, standing here acting like some jilted lover when they hadn't actually been lovers at all. It had just been a coincidence and he should be pleased Trisha was letting the whole thing go. The situation could have been humiliating. They could have shown up at work and discovered they couldn't work together at all. He had to admit, the fear had rushed through him on more than one occasion. Some of those chats had been heated, well beyond anything he would have said had he known he'd end up facing Trisha some day.

He'd been nervous, wondering how they would manage. But like always, Trisha's relaxed demeanor had put him at ease, and before he knew it, they were back to normal. He should be grateful and relieved, instead of mournful and sad.

So, why wasn't he?

"How's Virginia taking the news?" Bill asked, pulling Logan from his thoughts.

He snorted. "I think she made a voodoo doll of me. I woke up this morning with an ache in my jaw." He held up a finger. "No, wait, that's from all the grinning."

The group erupted with laughter, all except for Trisha and Adrienne who had gone to a corner of the room and were conducting a private conversation while they casually surveyed the scene. He squinted, trying to read their lips and decipher the subject, but he couldn't make out a thing.

"So," Adrienne said under her breath. "Three days in the Caribbean, just you and Logan. Sounds like a honeymoon to me."

Trisha replied between clenched teeth. "It's a business meeting and the Tyndales will be there. There won't be room for fun and frolic."

"There's always room for fun and frolic."

Trisha shook her head lightly. "It's too soon. I've got to show Logan I can do the job. Besides, he's just promoted me. If I go clawing after him now, he'll get the wrong impression and the whole thing will blow up in my face."

"You know what your problem is?" Adrienne said, raising her can of soda to her lips. "You think too much. You're overanalyzing this." She took a sip then spoke in a whisper, "The guy kissed you once. How big of a hint do you need?"

"This is our first business trip. I need to show him we can work together no matter where we are."

Adrienne blew out a quiet breath of fluster. "Fine. Do it your way. But I'm telling you, you drag this on too long, I'm going to seriously lose my patience."

The two women stood for a moment, silently watching the crowd and sipping their drinks. Trisha spotted Norah Germaine standing by the video unit and eyeing Logan's body as if she were pondering the selections on a dessert cart. Trisha wondered if the tall redhead had ever sauntered her way into Logan's bed, but immediately dismissed the thought. Knowing Norah, if she had, she would have plastered the news all over town and slapped a big "taken" sign on Logan's forehead.

She watched the woman practically lick her lips as she eyed a path down Logan's chest. Logan just stood, talking to Bill, oblivious of the vulture who was contemplating which piece of him she'd like to sample first.

"I'm bringing my beaded dress," she finally said.

Adrienne shot a side glance to Trisha, her eyes lit with an evil smile. "The blue one?"

Trisha flicked a brow. "I said I wouldn't make a pass. I never said I wasn't going to test the waters."

"You'll bring him to his knees."

"I certainly hope so."

"GUESS WHO I ran into yesterday?"

Logan glanced at Bill. "Who?" he asked.

"Sarah Jacobs."

"Hmm. I haven't seen her in years."

"She's divorced. Made a big point of letting me know that."

The news took Logan by surprise. He hadn't heard of any rumblings in the Jacobs household. "Really?" he asked. "What happened?"

"She didn't say. She spent most of the conversation asking about you."

Logan turned the thought over in his mind. He and Sarah had been acquainted since their days at U.C. San Francisco, and though he hadn't seen her in years, he remembered he'd always liked her. She was smart, attractive and fun to be around. And she could be just what he needed to get his mind off Trisha Bain.

"She still with Century Mortgage?" he asked.

"Yep. Made a big point of letting me know that, too. I got the distinct impression she's carrying a torch for you."

Bill chuckled as if the notion was ludicrous, but Logan had different ideas. Scorpio was gone and Trisha had clearly put their trysts behind her. Besides, he'd learned his lesson when it came to women in advertising, especially women who worked for his firm. Maybe it was time to put the past behind *him* and start with someone new. He and Sarah had always gotten along well. And though the woman never stirred his desire the way Trisha had, maybe that would come in time, if he gave it a chance.

Logan turned his eyes back to Trisha who was now smiling and whispering something in Devon's ear. She had a hand on his arm and Logan didn't expect the heat of jealousy her touch erupted.

He did need to get over Trisha before he did something foolish. Maybe Sarah was the way to do it.

Devon threw his head back and laughed, and Logan tightened his grip on his glass. What the hell had she said? Envy narrowed his eyes as he watched the two converse. Devon dipped his head to Trisha's ear and whispered something back. She smiled and nodded, then the two set down their glasses and proceeded to cross the room.

Her eyes met Logan's and a rush of embarrassment flushed his cheeks. Had he been obviously studying her? Her casual glance didn't say either way, but as the two moved toward him, he cleared his throat and forced a casual stance.

"Thank you for this," she said, extending a hand and a pleasant smile.

He pressed his palm to hers, feeling a wave of tingles burst where they touched. "You deserve it," he replied, quickly releasing his grasp.

"We've got an early flight. Why don't you go home?" he added, tucking his hand in his pocket.

"I will. I'm just going to go over a few things with Devon, then I'm off."

He glanced at Devon, the tall blonde looking thoroughly absent of any attraction to Trisha. Logan inwardly sighed. What was wrong with him? Trisha and Devon were just coworkers and if he wasn't mistaken, Devon was engaged to his long-time girlfriend.

Logan took a breath and relaxed. "I'll see you tomorrow then." He nodded goodbye as Trisha and Devon stepped out the door.

He seriously needed to get a grip on the situation before he drove himself insane. Trisha was moving on with her life, putting the secret they shared in the past. He should be pleased the affair hadn't driven a wedge between them. Things were returning to business as usual, his plan for Tyndale working exactly as he'd hoped. He had everything to be thankful for and instead of standing around acting like a spurned lover, he should be taking Trisha's lead and forgetting the whole situation with LoveSigns ever happened.

LOGAN STRETCHED HIS LEGS in front of him. He and Trisha had been flying for too many hours, and despite the first-class accommodations, his muscles were cramping.

Trisha, on the other hand, hadn't a care in the world. She simply continued to go through the materials Marc had given them on his new Cable Beach resort.

"These reports are fantastic. Their systems are more sophisticated than I'd expected. We'll be able to do quite a bit of data mining with all the stats they collect."

She pulled several brochures from the portfolio Tyndale had provided, holding them up in front of him. "But these brochures haven't been updated in years. Look at the hairstyles of the women in the photos. It's completely yesterday, not to mention borderline lewd."

Making notes on the pad on her lap, she mumbled, "So, in addition to what's already scheduled, I'll add in IT. I want to see what format we can get this data in and how many years back they've got. Some trend analysis would be helpful. Can you think of anything else?"

Honestly, he couldn't think about anything with her bare arm brushing against his elbow and that lavender scent swirling through his senses. He'd spent way too much time in close proximity to Trisha today, and he looked at his watch, relieved to find they were only a half hour from their destination.

"Not at the moment," he said.

She nodded then touched the pen to her lips. "I'll need to tour the surrounding area tomorrow. I've never been to the Bahamas and to get a real feel—"

"Trisha," he interrupted.

She stopped and glanced at him, those pale blue eyes sparkling in a way that twisted a knot in his stomach.

He snatched the folder from her hand and shoved it in her briefcase. "Stop talking about work. You've practically got the entire campaign laid out and we haven't even touched ground yet."

She sucked in a deep breath and exhaled. "Sorry."

"Tell me something personal. Like—" He thought for a moment. "What do your parents do?"

"Well, my mother is president of Sunwest Bank and my father is a professor at Berkeley."

"Your mother's a bank president? Why didn't I know that?"

"You never asked."

He considered and realized he'd never actually taken the time to get to know Trisha the way he had his other staff.

"And she always worked?" he asked. "Even when you were young?"

"Sure. I mean, she was just a bank manager when us kids were little. She didn't make the executive suite until I was in high school. But yeah, she always worked."

She settled in her seat as a spark of admiration lit in her eyes. "My mom's the best. I always thought she was so beautiful, showing up at school in those suits and heels. Sophisticated, you know? I'm so proud of her, accomplishing so much in her life, raising three kids, keeping the house and making a success of her career."

Logan found the fondness in her tone contagious. He could tell by the look in her eyes she was enamored with her mother.

"Is that what you want from life?"

"Yes."

There was no hesitation in her answer. Logan got the impression Trisha had a plan for herself that detailed exactly what she wanted and where she was going.

"It's not always easy to juggle family and a career," he said.

"Well, I think it's easier these days than it was when we were young. And my father worked odd hours. He never had classes all day. He did most of his work out of our home, so he was around for us. I guess that's something I'll have to consider when I find the right man."

Logan tried to fend off the sense of warmth he felt listening to Trisha talk about settling down and wanting a family and he couldn't help the tug of remorse when she talked about finding the right man. A side of him wanted to be that man, if only she were the right woman.

AFTER TRAVELING ALL DAY, the two finally made their way into the hotel lobby just before sundown. Logan was beat, and by the looks of Trisha, she was, too. Her eyes had grown heavy and what was once a perfect braid coiling down to her shoulder had now become a loose tousle of silky brown hair. Several strands fell haphazardly around her face. He actually liked the look. It was more casual, less refined and completely sexy. His mind had just trailed off to a vision of releasing the rest of the braid when he heard her gasp in awe.

"My God. Marble for as far as the eye can see. Those old brochures don't do this justice."

He took his eyes off her to study the lobby. It was remarkably plush and spacious and like Trisha said, acres of marble spanned the great open room. Even the palm trees that dotted the lobby seemed like house plants in the vast expanse.

They crossed to the desk and provided their information. After checking them in, the reservations clerk slid two key cards across the counter.

Logan noticed Trisha's eyes widen as she looked at the matching room numbers on the cards. Kelly had booked the standard two-bedroom suite, a habit he'd gotten into while traveling with Bill. It was easier to strategize with a central living area where they could spread out papers and go over ideas instead of looking for a conference room or taking over one of their rooms.

It had worked well for him and Bill, but Trisha didn't seem at all pleased.

"I'm sorry," he said. "Kelly booked a two-bedroom suite out of habit. We can change that if you'd like."

She flashed him a nervous smile and tried to pretend she hadn't been paying attention. "No, that's fine."

"You're sure?"

Her smile relaxed. "It's fine."

Shrugging it off, he crossed to the elevators. He could see Trisha's mind calculating the details of their ad campaign as they passed through the spacious room. She was taking in every aspect of the hotel, mentally picking and choosing which feature should hold most prominence when she put together the ads.

He pressed the button to their floor and watched her scan the space. Even the elevator compartment received a once-over as they rose. She stopped at every turn, studied every hallway as they made their way to the room and finally, Logan had seen enough.

"Give it a rest. You'll have plenty of time to work tomorrow."

Her cheeks turned a light shade of pink, but the hue deepened when he opened the door and led her into the room. The light smile that had curved her lips flattened when she stepped in and absorbed the surroundings. The look on her face was nothing short of terror and Logan knew exactly why.

If he were to draw a picture of the beach fantasy chat between Pisces and Scorpio, this would be the room, from the balcony and sheer curtains, right down to the chill from the air-conditioning.

His mind instantly flashed to their tropical interlude and he couldn't help but wonder if Trisha owned a blue-satin thong.

He shook the image away before an erection threatened embarrassment, but judging by the way Trisha stepped through the room, she hadn't stopped reliving every word of their chat.

Most women would have headed straight for the grand balcony to explore the view, but Trisha avoided the area as if it were haunted. Her intent to explore the hotel vanished as she diverted her eyes from every corner of the room, choosing instead to keep them planted firmly on the floor.

He stifled a smile. Apparently, Trisha hadn't brushed off Pisces as quickly as he'd suspected.

"Well, this will be comfortable," he said, trying to break the silence that had come over them.

She refused to meet his gaze. "My room. Where is my room?"

He tried to catch a glance of her face, but she kept turning away from him, allowing him only a glimpse of one strawberry-red cheek.

He pointed to the doors that opened on each side of the room. "Take whichever one you want."

She darted to the closest, muttering something about needing to change, but Logan couldn't hear the end of the statement. She'd disappeared into the room and shut the door behind her before he could open his mouth to utter a word.

Suddenly left alone, he opted for his bedroom, taking the time to hang up his suits and to clean up from the trip. It felt good to wash cool water over his face and remove his suit jacket and tie. When he emerged, Trisha's door was still shut, so he moved to the bar and poured himself a drink.

He checked his watch. Nearly an hour had passed and Trisha was still tucked away. He glanced over and noticed her suitcase sitting by the door. Growing concerned, he stepped over and rapped on the door.

"Trisha? Are you okay?"

There was no answer.

He pressed an ear to the door, but he couldn't hear the spray of a shower. She must have heard him.

He rapped again.

"Trisha?" he said, raising his voice.

Nothing. Maybe she'd fallen asleep. It had been a long day and he was rather tired himself. Carefully, he turned the knob and cracked open the door just to be sure.

The sight gave him a start. Trisha stood at the open window, clutching her arms across her chest. She hadn't so much as kicked off her shoes. By the looks of things, she'd simply tossed her briefcase and purse on the chair and stepped straight to the window where she'd remained for the past fifty minutes.

"Trisha," he said, causing her to jump and spin.

"Wha—?" she started, obviously disoriented.

"I was calling for you. Are you okay?"

Her chest pumped with quick breaths and her eyes were wide, bordering on crazed. A smile broke through the look of shock on her face, but he could see it was nothing more than a cover.

"I'm sorry. I didn't hear you."

He took a few steps into the room, being careful not to come too close. She was clearly on edge, ready to lose it.

"You've been standing there all this time?"

Her mouth bobbed before she finally replied, "I guess I lost track of time."

"You're a million miles away. What's wrong?"

She looked at him as though the situation should be obvious, glancing to the door then back to his chest. She wouldn't make eye contact, and by the look on her face, one wrong move would send her flying out of her shoes.

"That…" she said. "That room…it's…" she trailed off.

A smile broke on his face. "Familiar?"

"Yes," she hissed.

He chuckled with relief and stepped to the edge of the bed.

"I'm glad you find it amusing," she said, her cheeks flushing into a deep shade of scarlet.

He sobered the laugh. "Actually, I'm relieved. I'd thought you'd all but forgotten about your chats with Pisces." He cleared his throat. "It was beginning to bruise my ego."

She took a step back, only stopping because she'd hit the edge of the window and couldn't go farther. Her arms still held a vise grip around her chest, and though he could understand her discomfort, he couldn't comprehend the reason for the severity.

"Trisha, this last week you've acted as if nothing happened between us. Why the sudden change?"

"I just…I was used to the office. I'd had practice."

"Practice?"

She let out a huff, apparently disgruntled by the fact that he didn't understand. She bit her lip, hesitating for a moment before finally asking, "During those chats. When you thought of Scorpio, did you imagine someone specific? You know, in your mind?"

Confused, he replied, "No. Not really. Scorpio was just…a made-up image, I guess. I'd never really formed anything terribly specific."

She lowered her eyes to the floor as the flush deepened in her cheeks. He tried to understand where she was going with the question and then a memory hit him like a slap in the chest.

The man. The off-limits man Scorpio had professed to love. Had she said she'd loved him? Or had she just said she'd wanted him? Either way, the sentiment was revealing and as more of their chats ran through his mind, his smile slowly faded. Had he been that ignorant, or had Trisha simply been that good at hiding her feelings?

Or was he completely misunderstanding her question, letting his ego control his thoughts?

His voice soft and cautious, he asked, "Who was Pisces for you?"

Without moving her eyes from the floor, she mumbled, "Isn't it obvious?"

Several emotions vied for prominence. Elation that Trisha had thought more of him than he'd realized, confusion when he tried to link her words with her actions this past week and fear over where this whole thing could end.

He wasn't sure what to focus on first. It had hurt him to think she'd so casually dismissed her relationship with Pisces. Since learning the truth, he hadn't been able to shake her from his mind and he didn't understand how she could have just gone on as if nothing had occurred. He'd gone so far as to think she was just another Virginia, but even Virginia couldn't have mustered the look of shame and embarrassment he was seeing right now.

"Trisha," he said, still not ready to absorb her words. "What were you doing on that Web site?"

She closed her eyes and swallowed hard. Her body trembled, her hands clamped tightly around her waist and just when he thought she wasn't going to answer the question, she opened her eyes and admitted, "Trying to get over you."

"Get over me?"

Shock pushed him back a step. Damn. She'd had a crush on him and never once did he see it. All this time, he'd been sulking, thinking he hadn't mattered, assuming the worst, when it was all right in front of his face. Trisha had wanted him, she'd just been too afraid to show it.

"This doesn't have to change our working relationship," she said. "I've just…had a moment here. It was… this room. It caught me off guard. But with a good night's sleep, I'll be fine."

She took a step toward him, the pain in her eyes easing, replaced by a look of determined assurance. "This doesn't have to change things."

Doesn't have to change things? On the contrary, it changed everything. Trisha may be capable of burying her emotions for the sake of her job, but he certainly couldn't. Once it had sunk in that she was Scorpio, Logan could barely think of anything else. He'd been so consumed by his desire for her, the only thing keeping him at bay was his notion that his feelings weren't returned.

And now Trisha had pulled the rug out from under him.

How could he turn and walk out? From the moment he'd found out about Scorpio, he hadn't been able to shake the feeling that Trisha belonged to him. He'd opened himself to her, shared a part of his heart he'd held captive for years.

He might have the strength to deny it today, but could he still tomorrow, and the next day and the day after that?

One look at those soft, dewy eyes and he knew the answer was no. Trisha had crept in from so many different angles he knew there was no releasing her now. She was his and every part of his body begged him to claim her once and for all.

"I can do this," she assured. "I can get over it."

"But I can't," he replied.

He stepped close, cupped her face in his hands and brushed his thumbs across her flushed cheeks. He could feel her tense in his hands, though she tried to hold on to control.

"Do you really think I can just forget about Scorpio?"

He studied her, watching the need, fear and joy swirl through her eyes like sparkling blue whirlpools, and in a final snap of desire, he dipped his head and crushed his mouth with hers.

The instant their lips touched, the tension drained from her limbs like sand through a sieve, and every part of his body came to life. Desire raged through him and he widened his mouth, wanting to take in more.

She collapsed against his chest, bringing her hands around his waist and trailing them up his back, sending shivers through his veins. Scorpio was his, and tonight, he wanted her fully.

His heart racing, his chest pounding, he wrapped his arms around her and pulled her closer and the moan that crept from her throat made him want to sing to the world. She'd wanted him as much as he'd wanted her and the notion opened the gate to a stampede of lust and hunger. For the first time in years his body felt alive. Trisha had awakened his heart, unleashed his need, and this time, there would be no hesitation.

He swept his hands over her, wanting to take in each luscious curve and tender mound until every part of her body was sealed firmly in his mind. He wanted to feel the flesh that he'd only been able to imagine. He wanted to taste her until she stayed on his lips forever. He wanted to breathe her scent, until she was fully absorbed in his soul.

His tongue circled hers with greed, probing and caressing while his hands roamed over her body. He lifted them to her hair, pulled the band from her braid and laced his fingers through the silky strands that had haunted him in the lobby. They spread over his wrists like ribbons of satin and he ached to feel them against his bare chest.

His erection throbbed, he needed her closer and no matter how far he sank into the embrace, it simply wasn't enough. He needed more than this moment. He needed more than just her lips. And though his body begged him to stay, he had no choice but to pull away. His breath ragged, his voice hoarse, he whispered into her mouth, "I want you, Trisha. All of you."

10

Daily Love Horoscope for Scorpio

> After a long, patient wait, the planets have finally
> aligned in your favor. But where is it all heading?
> Who cares?! Sit back and enjoy the vacation. You've
> waited too long to do anything less.

LOGAN'S WORDS shot like lightning through Trisha's veins.

He wanted her. He wanted all of her. And the thirst
in his kiss told her this time he wouldn't pull back.

Her thoughts began spinning in circles, fueled by the
greed of his touch and the fire in his eyes. This wasn't
the Logan she knew, the man who had steadily proclaimed his interest in her was strictly professional,
the man who, before Scorpio, hadn't shown the slightest spark of attraction to her.

Before Scorpio.

The thought circled back in her mind. Who exactly
did Logan want, Trisha or Scorpio? And being they
were one and the same, did it even matter?

His hands brushed over her breasts, sending a flurry
of sensation to her sex, clouding her rational mind.

He wanted her, and she wanted him, too. She wanted Logan and Pisces, and for her, the two had always been one. But that wasn't the case for Logan. He hadn't expressed any desire for Trisha. Not until he'd learned the truth about LoveSigns.

But did it matter? she wondered again, trying to shake her senses out of this cluster of lust and need. She had to protect her heart, but with every squeeze of his hands to her flesh, every hot press of his lips to her neck, her will kept losing the battle against desire.

"Tell me you want me, too, baby," he said, sucking the lobe of her ear between his lips.

"Yes," she hissed, the guttural response fleeing from her mouth before her mind could truly contemplate an answer. She did want him, she always had, and as his hands began pulling the blouse from her slacks, she decided nothing else mattered. She *was* Scorpio, and if it was LoveSigns that pushed him into her arms, she'd take it and run.

Their hands flew into motion, snatching at buttons and clasps while his mouth clamored at the sensitive skin of her throat. She worked fast to remove his shirt, to expose the chest she'd forever dreamed of touching.

So many times, she'd ached to place her palms to his chest, to feel the dense muscles and capture the heat against her fingers and let the soothing beat of his heart pulse against her breasts. She wanted to rid the barriers that had stood between them, to shed hesitancy, fear and reluctance with every drape of clothing that fell to the floor.

Tonight, she wanted him wholly, to take and be taken, until everything standing between them dissolved and every inch of their bodies was explored.

She did want him. Be it Logan with Trisha, or Pisces with Scorpio, the answer remained the same. She wanted the man in her arms as much as she wanted her next breath.

Piece by piece, clothes pooled at their feet, a symbol of doubt abandoned and with every layer they shed, her desire deepened. She unhooked her bra, allowing the pout of her breasts to fall into his waiting hands and a slow groan of pleasure seeped from his throat.

And through that one weary groan, the tender brush of his thumbs, the warm suckling of his mouth, she felt that pure and utter beauty Pisces had always brought to their chats.

It had been his draw. Somehow, through their chats, the man had made her feel beautiful, as if their lovemaking left no room for modesty. Only with Pisces had she felt pure, untainted by insecurity and laced with true passion.

Logan. Logan Moore was Pisces and reliving those chats in the flesh did nothing to dispel that feeling. He touched as if her body was a work of fine art, his eyes spoke words of admiration and affection and with every press of his lips, the fire grew hotter, blazing away her inhibitions just like Pisces had done with words so many times before.

She trailed her hands up his chest, over his shoulders and down his muscled arms, the pleasure in the touch reminding her this was real. Logan was a living, breathing soul, spilling life into every corner of her body.

His breath puffed against her skin, surrounding her

in a mist of desire, and when he held her waist and pulled her near, she gasped at the hardness of his erection pressing against her.

"Do you know how much I've wanted this?" he whispered to her ear.

"No," she said, her voice raspy and full of longing.

"I can't count the times I've wanted to take you in my office," he said, trailing more kisses down her throat. "So many times I've wanted to crawl through that damned computer and show you what I can do for you, instead of typing the words on the keyboard."

His admission weakened her legs and snatched the breath from her lungs. "Show me now, Logan," she whispered.

As if she'd spoken the final words of acceptance, he reached down and took her into his arms, crossed the room and laid her on the bed, pausing a moment to study her body. His stiff cock underscored the look of need in his gaze, and the deep flames in his eyes brought her to a feverish peak. This was really happening between them, and once again, she had to mentally regroup to believe it was true.

He knelt and spread his body next to hers, pulling her against him, allowing his hard length to brush between her legs and the sensation sent a hot rush of wetness to her core. The ache began to build as his mouth trailed over her shoulder and down to her breast.

"You're so beautiful, Trisha." His voice was low and husky. "My body wants you fast, but my mind wants to savor every moment."

She smiled, thinking he'd taken the words from her

mouth. Taking his face in her hands, she raised his eyes to hers.

"This isn't your one and only chance, you know."

He smiled back, cupping her cheek and stroking his fingers through her hair. "No," he said, pressing a kiss to her lips. "I have many plans for you."

He lowered his mouth over hers and swept a finger between her folds, sending a searing burst of pleasure through her. She stiffened in his arms, the sensation threatening to send her cascading over the edge with one swift stroke.

"Oh," he groaned, sliding a finger into her center. "You're so wet."

Trisha couldn't reply. Pulsing waves ripped through her as he slid another finger inside, the ache in his groan matching the torment in her chest. Her breath grew heavy and tiny beads of sweat pooled on her skin. His hard, naked body caressed over hers, sending heat through her veins as she clasped her hands against his firm, hot chest.

He gently stroked his thumb over her clit, massaging wave after wave of pleasure until her center throbbed. She squirmed in his arms, her need to have him inside warring with her need for swift release.

"Where's that spot, sweetheart?"

He moved his thumb to one side and began to explore.

"No," was all she could say. His light, musky scent cloaked her senses, his breath dusted like feathers against her skin. Her center ached, her heart thundered, but she didn't want it to end like this. She wanted all of him. She wanted his hardness to fill her. She wanted to taste his mouth on hers and to feel his climax while the weight of his body made this all truly real.

He shifted his thumb, sending a quick burst of sensation through her spine. She arched her back and cried out, and a dark, knowing smile curved his lips.

"There it is," he said, his chuckle of delight flushing her cheeks with frustration.

"No," she begged. "I want you inside."

He lowered his head and put his mouth to her breast, brushing his tongue over her nipple before pulling back and blowing breath over the moistened spot, sending her body in a swirl of light shivers.

"You'll have that, too, baby. Just let go."

He slid his mouth to her other breast and brushed his thumb over the spot, sending her spinning toward the edge. She brought her hands to his head and trailed her fingers through the soft curls that she'd wanted to touch so often. There were so many things she wanted to feel and taste, but it was all moving too fast. She tried to hold on, wanting to get him inside before her body swept off without him, but one final brush of his thumb brought the climax raging through her.

She writhed in his arms while her hands clutched his mouth against her breast. Sharp sprays of light flashed like a strobe before her eyes, and through his low groan of victory, she heard herself cry out.

He lightened his touch, widening the caress away from her center as the climax brushed like satin over her skin. Her limbs went numb, her body sunk into the bed and without realizing he had moved, she looked up to see him sheathing his cock as he hovered intently over her.

LOGAN LOOKED DOWN at Trisha, thinking he'd never seen such beauty. Sweat glistened on her skin, giving her the luster of a finely cultured pearl. Her eyes were moist and sated and the rose in her cheeks mirrored that of a porcelain doll.

Never had he gained such pleasure feeling a woman shatter in his arms, and at that moment, he knew he'd want to feel that sensation again and again.

Scorpio. His tender Scorpio was laced with more fire and passion than could ever be conveyed on the screen and his body told him it was time to take everything she had to give.

He lowered over her, relishing the feel of her against him. Trisha's body. The form that had driven him mad by day, heated with the fire Scorpio had exuded at night. The two came together in a package he knew he could never deny, and as he slowly slid inside, the glory in her eyes colored every part of his soul.

She slipped her hands around his neck and pressed her mouth to his, the sweet taste of her lips branding him as her sweet lavender scent cloaked his senses in desire. She inhaled a deep breath as he slid farther, her soft purrs telling him he had everything she needed to send her over again and the knowledge filled him with a sense of sheer valor.

Slowly, they stroked, their movements working together like a finely tuned machine, sending sparks twirling from his loin through his chest. He propped up on his elbows, wanting to study the pleasure on her face. Those gray flecks in her pale blue eyes sparkled like sunlight on a tropical sea and the words those eyes conveyed stole a piece of his heart.

God, she was beautiful.

And now she was his.

Wave after wave crested until he felt his shaft swell and his hands begin to tremble. He wanted to hold on. He wanted to feel her climax around him, but as more bursts tore through him, he doubted he could last.

Trisha's eyes grew dark, her breath returned to pants and when her hands gripped his waist and pulled him deeper, he nearly lost control.

"Go, honey. Let go," he urged, his deep focus trying to convey there wasn't much time.

"Faster," she said, jutting her hips in a motion that pushed his climax straight to the edge.

He closed his eyes. He needed to hold on, but the silky brush of her core unraveled him with every quick stroke.

Just as he was about to concede defeat and find his release, a gasp from her lungs caused him to open his eyes in time to watch her shatter. She curved her back and buried her face in his chest as her core clamped tightly around his shaft. Her body quivering, her hips thrusting, he had no choice but to catch the wave and ride along.

The orgasm swept through his chest and burst in a fierce spray of light and for a moment, he had no idea where he was or what would happen. Her muffled cries echoed in his ears and her fingers dug into his flesh as the climax sent him into a torment of spasms.

It ripped and quaked through him, stealing control

of his motion until finally his muscles gave out and he collapsed on her chest. Sinking his face in the crook of her neck, he tried to relax his heavy breath. His heart beat fast, yet for what seemed like forever, he couldn't move so much as a toe.

Her light giggle vibrated against his chest, causing him to raise up from her. The serenity in her eyes spoke volumes, but he couldn't help asking the question.

"How do you feel?"

A seductive smile curved her rosy lips. "Excellent."

"Hmm. Scorpio always just said good."

She circled her arms around his neck. "Scorpio never had you in the flesh."

"No," he chuckled. He lifted off her chest, but she tightened her grasp and yanked him back.

"Don't go."

"I'm crushing you."

She shook her head and smiled. "No, you're not. I like it."

"You like suffocating?"

She pressed a kiss to his chin. "I like the weight of your body on mine. It helps remind me that you're real."

A warm smile sprouted in his chest and bloomed across his lips. He understood the sentiment, but he couldn't get past the notion that he was too heavy for the slender woman in his arms. Rolling onto his back, he slipped his arm around her, inviting her to nestle against him. Her silky hair draped like satin over his shoulder, and as her slim fingers glided in circles around his chest, he raised them to his lips and warmed them with a kiss.

"Did you really fantasize about making love to me in your office?" she asked.

Logan studied the inquisitive look in her eyes. "Wasn't that the premise of just about all our chats?"

She smiled, but the grin held a hint of reluctance. "Not Scorpio," she finally said. "Me. Trisha."

He crunched his brow into a frown and rolled onto his side to face her. Brushing chestnut tresses from her face, he replied, "You are Scorpio. You always were."

"But you said…" She trailed off.

"Who do you think inspired that navy-blue skirt?"

A twinkle brightened her eyes.

He sighed and pulled her close. "Every time you wore it, I thought I might break down and take you right there in the office." Looking down, he flashed a pained grin. "Please, tell me you weren't really naked underneath."

Her cheeks flushed to a deep shade of fuchsia. Through a giggle, she admitted, "Once."

His mouth fell open. "You're kidding me."

She shook her head as her fuchsia cheeks deepened to scarlet.

"When? No." He held up a hand. "I don't even want to know. It's too painful to consider." He cupped the back of her neck and pressed a light kiss to her lips. "Just promise me you'll let me know the next time."

He studied her smile, still not seeing the satisfaction he had hoped for. Tucking a finger under her chin, he lifted her gaze to his.

"What?" he asked.

"You never gave me the slightest sign. I thought I was the last person you'd be interested in."

He nearly laughed out loud. "Kissing you in your office wasn't a sign?"

Realization relaxed the tension in her brow, but only slightly. He huffed, accepting the fact that he'd done a bang-up job sending her mixed signals. While his needs had battled his fears, Trisha obviously ended up a casualty and it was officially time to rid this relationship of all misunderstandings between them.

"Do you know that you have exactly seven gray flecks in your eyes?" he asked.

Her expression turned shocked and confused.

"I counted them. There's three on the right and four on the left."

"You counted the flecks in my eyes?"

"It was that or kiss you at your doorway."

Now she was looking at him as though she thought he could be insane. He figured he might as well dispel the question.

"You also twitch your nose when you don't know the answer to a question," he added, propping his head in his hand. "You bite your lip when you want something, especially when that something is chocolate. You wear your hair up on Wednesdays and Fridays, although I never knew why."

"Those are the mornings I work out."

He nodded. "Ah, that fits." He thought for a second, trying to conjure up more Trisha nuances he'd stored in his memory. "You have a tiny mole above your left ankle, you take exactly two creams in your coffee and when you cross your legs, it's always right over left."

"I can't believe you noticed all that."

He sighed and cocked his mouth in a half-smile. "Yes, apparently I noticed everything but the giant elephant standing in the middle of the room."

He finally saw the warm glow of relief calm the worry from her face. Pulling her close, he pressed a kiss to her forehead.

"I think it's time we stop hiding our feelings, don't you?"

TRISHA COULDN'T THINK of anything she'd rather do. These last few weeks had been such a whirlwind, she still had trouble believing she was actually in bed with Logan, naked, sharing secrets after an incredible bout of sex. Any moment, she expected to wake up and find herself back on the airplane, disappointment crushing her hopes when she realized it was all just a dream.

And now she was hearing how much he'd always wanted her, how many ways he'd studied her and stored her quirks in his memory. It looked as though neither of them had noticed the mutual attraction between them. Either that, or they were both terribly adept at concealing their deepest desires. No wonder they both sought release through LoveSigns. It took a lot of energy to remain so controlled.

"No more hiding," she agreed, shifting into the embrace.

She couldn't keep her hands from roaming his chest, seeking that constant assurance that they were really here, in the flesh, admitting their desire for each other. It was almost too much to absorb and she wondered if she'd ever get used to the idea that they might actually be an item.

"This all seems very surreal," she said.

"Hmm. I wouldn't have chosen that word."

She looked up at his eyes. "No?"

"No. I would have chosen something closer to ec-stasy. And to think," he added, pulling her closer. "We haven't even checked out the balcony yet."

She gasped at the suggestion. "That beach isn't deserted."

Logan's low, husky laugh rumbled against her chest. It was the laugh she'd always envisioned hearing in a situation like this—deep, sensual and filled with de-lightfully evil connotations.

"Okay," he said. "That's your first assignment as vice president of travel when we get back to the office. Find us a deserted beach."

Trisha didn't know why, but hearing Logan talk about their future left her pleasantly surprised. She hadn't thought beyond this moment, much less what they would do when they returned home. She wanted to ask for his thoughts, whether he wanted to keep this a secret, whether he truly wanted this to continue, but she swept the urge away. She'd finally got him where she wanted him, heard the words she'd dreamed of hearing, experienced the sex she'd ached to enjoy. This was the moment to simply bask in that pleasure.

"Well," he said, brushing his hardening cock against her waist. "Balcony or no balcony, I'm certain there are a few chats we can revisit before the week-end is out."

An evil smile crossed her lips. Logan had the right frame of mind and despite her wanting to consider their future, she resolved to spend every minute enjoying the weekend—starting right now.

Pushing him onto his back, she moved her body over his, discarded the condom and took him in her hand.

"Actually," she said. "I've got some new ideas I'd like to run by you."

He lifted one eyebrow, intrigued.

Putting a hand to his thigh, she said, "Come on, make yourself comfortable."

There was no hesitation in his movement as he shuffled back and leaned against the plush, cushioned headboard. Trisha handed him a pillow.

"Really comfortable."

His dark eyes lit with pleasure and interest as he adjusted the pillow behind him and did as he was told. Trisha took a breath and exhaled any remnants of fear and contemplation she'd been holding. From this moment on, she would relish every moment, explore every curve and give herself freely to Logan's deepest whim.

Gently, she cradled his sac in one hand and used her other to caress the silky texture of his cock, feeling the pang of excitement when it stiffened to attention in her hand. She trailed a light touch around the soft curve of the head, down the shaft and back again, noting every small peak and valley along the way. She threaded her fingers through the curls of his loin, allowing the wisps to prick at her skin while she watched his erection pulse from the touch.

Needing to get closer, she shifted her position, bending down to put the tip of his cock in her mouth, and when she did, a low growl strummed in Logan's chest.

She used her tongue to trace the path she'd just made with her fingers, and when she was done, she took the head in her mouth, sucking it in and lapping at the pulsing vein of his shaft.

She closed her eyes, wanting to heighten her other senses, concentrating her focus on touch, sound and the distinct scent of sex. His smooth shaft grew with every brush of her tongue, his breath slowed and deepened through the low moan in his throat. His fingers lightly caressed her hair as he whispered words of pleasure and acceptance.

And with every new moan, every tender word, her sense of power and freedom emerged.

Never had Trisha taken such pleasure in giving herself to a man. Maybe it was Logan's selflessness when it came to making love, maybe it was the casual freedom he portrayed, the sense that there were no boundaries when it came to sharing their bodies. Or maybe it was the intense satisfaction in knowing she could give the man of her dreams everything he could possibly desire.

Whatever the reason, she knew this place was hers, for however long it lasted and she intended to give and take as much pleasure as two souls could combine.

She gradually quickened her pace, his throbbing erection feeding heat to her sex, but as his breath became more ragged, his hands came down around her and urged her up. She opened her eyes as he pulled his cock from her mouth, and what she saw in his gaze left her startled.

Logan had never looked at her with such a profound

sense of affection and if she hadn't known better, what she saw in his eyes might actually have been love.

"Straddle me, honey," he whispered, grabbing a condom from the bedside table. "I want my hands on you."

She obliged, rolling the rubber onto his shaft then settling over him until he was buried deep inside. Her already throbbing clit grew hotter as she rocked and moved over him, his hands caressing up her waist and across her breasts with a touch as light as silk.

Slowly, she increased the stroke, watching his brown eyes darken, his breath quicken, before he clasped her shoulders and pulled her to his chest.

He pressed his lips to her cheek and clamped on to her waist, deepening the stroke, pumping harder and faster until she thought she'd burst in his arms.

"You drive me crazy, Trisha," he said in a voice hoarse with need.

The greedy desperation in his tone filled her heart and sent her body teetering on the edge.

"I'm going, baby. I'm going fast," he warned. And with two more strokes, he cupped her face in his hands, crushed his lips to hers and cried his release in her mouth.

Trisha quickly followed, the orgasm cresting hard until her arms failed her and she collapsed against his chest. Her breath came in short puffs, her body pulsed around his shaft and all she could do was rest in his arms while he covered her face with warm kisses.

He brought his arms around her and held her tight, and the clutch of his embrace told her he didn't want to let go. Which was just fine with her. There was nowhere else in the world she cared to be, and as they lay quietly, she felt her world shift into place.

He pressed his lips to her hair and murmured, "Every time I think I'm in heaven, you just take me higher."

Lifting her head from his shoulder, she sank into his gaze and smiled.

11

ADRIENNE STEPPED OUT of the bath and dried off, dreading what she'd find when she slipped on a robe and walked toward her living room. Bill was in the midst of orchestrating an incredible evening for them that started with dinner at Macca's, one of San Francisco's trendiest new restaurants. Next was a carriage ride down by the wharf and when they'd returned to her apartment, he'd drawn a warm bubble bath and insisted she relax while he "took care of some things."

It was a night most women would dream of. A night that was special with a capital *S*.

And that's exactly what worried her.

She knew Bill. The man had never been a romantic, which had always worked for her. She was the type who preferred a ball game over dinner and dancing, or a long hike in the woods to a candlelit dinner with roses and violins.

But it wasn't his choice of activity that gave her concern. It was where it might be leading.

This was the kind of night that had marriage proposal written all over it, and as she draped the towel on the rod and reached for her robe, she closed her eyes and silently prayed she was wrong. Since learning she was pregnant, she'd been literally torn in two between Bill's expectations and her parents' prodding. The two were on opposite sides of the social spectrum, and Adrienne, floating somewhere in the middle, had become the rope in a virtual tug-of-war. Add a poorly motivated marriage proposal to the mix and all she could think about was sneaking off to a deserted island where she could spend the next eight months enjoying her pregnancy in peace.

She'd spent nearly an hour in the tub, rehearsing what she would say if her fears came true, and no matter how many kind words she conceived, Bill's reaction wasn't playing well in her mind. "No" was never an answer he accepted with grace and she knew no matter how she tried to sugar-coat her words, rejecting his proposal would not go over well.

But it was a proposal she couldn't accept. Not now. Not like this. Sure, Bill might think he loved her, but she couldn't get past the notion that he was more in love with his child than its mother. Or worse, he wasn't crazy about either, he was just doing what he felt was right.

"Hon, you just about done?"

Her heart dropped a notch at the sound of Bill's voice. She didn't want to go out there, afraid of what she might find. Out of sheer reaction, her eyes darted around the bathroom, as if somewhere among the tiles she might find an escape. But giving in to the inevitable, she forced a cheerful reply.

"Coming right out."

She tucked her arms in the silky robe and tied the sash around her waist, then reluctantly stepped into the hall. Padding down the wood floor, she tried to lift her spirits. She could be wrong, after all. Bill could just be showing her a nice evening for no reason at all. It was highly possible her flippant hormones were just playing tricks on her, making her imagine all kinds of ridiculous things.

But when she stepped into the living room and took in the scene before her, her hopes went down the drain.

The room was filled with roses, lit with what must have been at least a dozen candles. Soft, New Age music spread over the room. She recognized it as Enya, one of the favorite CDs she turned to when she wanted quiet relaxation and his gesture clenched tightly around her throat. Bill didn't care for what he called her "yogi-guru" music, but somewhere along the line, he'd taken the time to note her favorite.

His face conveyed a warm sense of anticipation that sank in her chest and brought a flood of tears to her eyes.

"Hey, what's wrong?" he asked, moving swiftly to take her hand. Oh, God, she was really crying, she thought, as she felt a tear slide down her cheek. She flushed with embarrassment, wondering if this pregnancy was going to permanently reduce her to a blubbering fool.

She sniffed. "This is just so sweet."

He chuckled and led her to the couch where a bottle of champagne sat on ice and two crystal flutes adorned the coffee table. She took a seat and pointed to the glasses.

"What's this?"

Bill relaxed next to her. Pulling the bottle from the bucket, he poured the sparkling wine into the flutes.

"We haven't celebrated the baby."

She blinked away her tears. "I shouldn't drink alcohol."

He smiled and nestled the bottle back into the ice. "Relax. It's nonalcoholic."

He touched his glass to hers, causing a small crystal chime to float through the air. His brown eyes charmed and tender, he led the toast. "To the mother of my child and the woman I hope to grow old with."

Her smile was shaken and brief and she concealed her nerves by lifting the glass to her lips and taking a sip. He took the glass from her hand, set it on the table and reached into his pocket, pulling out a black velvet box. She stared at the case as if it were a poisonous insect, her hands trembling as she realized her fears had come true.

"Wha-what is that?"

He smiled, his eyes dark and glistening in the soft candle light. "What do you think it is?" Bill took her hand in his. "Adie, I want our life together to start out right."

He moved to open the box, but she covered his hand with hers. "Bill, don't."

That was all it took to drain the dimpled smile from his face.

"Please," she continued. "This isn't the way."

"This isn't the way to what?"

"To make our lives start out right."

Confusion pursed his brow. "Adie, I love you. You're having my child."

Lifting the lid on the box, he displayed a diamond ring, an emerald-cut solitaire that brought the tears back to her eyes. It was stunning, exactly the ring she would have chosen for herself, simple yet unique. Just another example of how well he knew her.

"I want you to be my wife."

Through the crush of despair, she tried to recall the words she'd rehearsed in the tub.

"Bill," she said, swallowing hard again. "I'd love to be your wife someday, but not now. Not like this."

She felt a slight breath of relief when she saw his eyes widen with shock. It was better than the hurt she'd expected.

"What do you mean, not like this?"

"Not just because of the baby."

His shock darkened to anger. "You think this is just for the baby?"

She blinked. "Yes."

"Ade, what part of 'I love you' don't you understand?"

"You never said those words before I got pregnant."

"Does that make it any less true?"

"No—I mean, yes." She took a breath, trying to collect her scattered thoughts. "I think you're confused."

He snapped the box closed and set it on the table, then brushed his hands over his face. She could see he hadn't expected this response and a side of her became angry that he hadn't. It was all so obvious to her, she couldn't fathom how he'd think she would just rush into his arms and squeal out a resounding, yes.

"I'm not confused," he said. "I want to marry the mother of my child."

"Exactly," she snapped. "The mother of your child. This is all about the baby. You wouldn't be considering this, or even talking about love, if I weren't pregnant."

"You don't know what you're talking about," he said with a sigh.

"Yes, I do. You're getting wrapped up in the idea of fatherhood, doing what you think is right."

"Is it so wrong to want to be a father to my child?"

"Bill." She raised a hand to his cheek, but he pushed it away and rose to pace the floor.

He pointed a finger at her. "My child's going to have a father. A *real* father. Not just some weekend dad."

"Of course."

"Not the way you're talking." He stuffed his hands in his pockets and quickened his pace. "What are you going to do, Ade, raise it here in the Haight?"

"I don't know."

"The city's no place for a child. We should be up in Marin near our folks, in a house with a yard, a safe neighborhood, good schools."

"Bill, there's plenty of time for all that."

He turned and stopped, the flicker of candlelight mirroring hot flames in his eyes. "When?"

"After the baby's born."

"What, when he's twelve?"

Her heart stepped up a beat. Of all the scenarios she'd expected, Bill's angry response wasn't one of them and now he was sinking to irrationality. She hated when he got this way and it was a stiff reminder why this notion of marriage was a bad idea.

"I need to take one thing at a time," she said, intentionally calming her voice to keep the situation from escalating.

He tilted his head and took on an inquisitive look. "Do you love me?"

Her mind numb from shock, she hesitated before stuttering, "I—I don't know."

A wash of hurt swept over his eyes and Adrienne immediately regretted her answer. Bill pulled his hands from his pockets and pressed his temples between his fingers.

"Oh, this is just great."

The speed of her pulse accelerated. "This has all been a lot to deal with. I don't know how I feel about anything and I certainly don't trust my emotions. That's my problem with this whole thing. I don't trust anything right now."

He raised his eyes to hers. "You don't trust me?"

"I…" She closed her eyes and took a breath to calm her nerves.

It didn't work.

"I don't trust that you really love me," she finally said.

He threw his hands in the air. "How many ways do I have to prove it to you?"

"You can start by backing off."

She quickly wished back the statement and the tone in which it was delivered. She was getting too flustered, her nerves were ready to split and the sharp look of offense on Bill's face wasn't helping.

She tried to regroup. "Bill, I'm not saying I don't love you. I'm not saying I'll never marry you. I'm just confused. I need time to sort things out."

"Fine," he said, grabbing his coat from the chair. "You need time, I'll give you time." He moved to the entryway and grasped to the doorknob. "You need me to back off," he said, pausing as a twitch of anger pursed his lips. "I'll back off."

He pulled open the door and stepped out, leaving her alone among the candles, roses and her diamond engagement ring.

LOGAN SLIPPED on his jacket and straightened his tie, preparing for dinner with the Tyndales. He and Trisha had spent an excruciatingly long day in their company touring the resort and discussing ideas for the campaign. Not that he didn't like Marc and Corinne. He just wasn't in the mood for touring anything other than the curves and crevices of Trisha's naked body now that he'd had her in his arms.

They'd managed to sneak in a quickie when they returned to the suite to shower and change for dinner. That was forty-five minutes ago, but if he went by the clock in his body, it might as well have been last week. He couldn't remember ever wanting a woman so deeply—and so often. No matter how many times they made love, it wasn't enough, and he wondered if it had to do with LoveSigns.

For months, the two had been enticing each other on that Web site, sharing sexual fantasies without the benefit of being able to carry them out in the flesh. It would be natural for a couple in their situation to have an exaggerated desire for each other. But as he looked in the mirror, the giddy grin staring back at him told him it was something more.

Was it love?

The notion straightened the smile on his face. He stared blankly at the mirror, trying to decide if that would be good or bad. It had been years since he'd felt this alive, experienced that fullness in his heart, that excitement to start each day. He liked the feeling, the way it lifted his spirits and sharpened his senses. But could he handle being devastated all over again if things ended badly?

Logan knew life was about taking risks. It wasn't worth living if you couldn't take a chance now and then. But some things were too risky, some stakes too high and he couldn't help but fear falling in love with Trisha was one of them.

What if his early suspicions about her were true? Could she really just be another Virginia, chasing after the boss to further her career? He'd appointed her vice president on her own merit, but how far up the ladder did she really want to go? She had just achieved the highest position he could offer at his firm, unless he made her a full partner and he had no intention of ever doing that. He'd already seen what that arrangement could cost him. He wasn't going to let anyone push him into making that mistake again, not even a woman he loved.

Which was exactly why he'd wanted to keep his love life out of the office. He'd known the complications he would encounter if he got involved with a woman at the firm, and somehow, during the last several days, he'd dismissed it. He'd shoved all apprehension under the rug when he'd learned the truth about Trisha and LoveSigns.

His mind returned to his chats with Scorpio, and he

quickly brushed off his doubts. Trisha wasn't Virginia. He and Trisha had delved into each other's hearts long before they'd known each other's identities. Scorpio wasn't after corporate success. During their chats, she'd rarely even mentioned her job, and through them, he'd learned she wanted more than just a career. She wanted a partner in life, the same thing he'd been looking for when he'd first married Virginia.

Scorpio wanted a soul mate, and long before he knew she was Trisha Bain, he'd felt as though he was that mate.

"Can I fix you a drink? We've got a little time."

He turned to see Trisha standing in the doorway and the sight drained the debate from his mind.

She wore her hair down, allowing the sleek, easy style to sweep over one eye, resting lightly on bare shoulders. He loved when she wore her hair down, the way a light breeze could catch the silky wisps and allow the sunlight to turn the dark russet strands into a deep caramel gold.

But it was the dress that stirred his blood and caused him to lose his train of thought. The striking sapphire-blue fabric hugged every curve from those full creamy breasts down to her tender, dimpled knees. Tiny silver beads wove a tapestry of shimmering roses, as if the designer had taken the color of her eyes and draped it over her body.

He opened his mouth to say something, but he couldn't conjure a compliment that did justice to her beauty.

Her face sobered with concern as she glanced down to her form. "What's wrong?"

"You expect me to talk business with you dressed like that?"

A smile relaxed her expression. "You'll be fine." Turning to step out, she tossed a glance over her shoulder. "How about a Tanqueray and tonic?"

That was the last thing he needed, liquor to dissolve the only morsel of inhibition he still held on to. He straightened the sleeves of his jacket and followed her out to the bar, taking a heavy breath to replace the air she'd managed to swipe from his lungs. Stepping close, he stifled the urge to touch her.

"You look stunning," he said. "I'd kiss you, but I fear if I did, we wouldn't make it down to dinner."

She grinned and handed him the drink. "You're insatiable."

"Exactly." He sipped his drink, allowing the sour lime taste to cleanse his lustful thoughts. "So, eat fast and fake a few yawns so we can be back here in an hour tops."

"We're supposed to be here on business."

He winked. "And I intend to get down to business just as soon as I get you out of that dress."

She tried to scoff, but it came out as a quirky smile. Unable to resist temptation, he slid a hand around her waist and pressed a kiss to her lips. The fruity taste of her mouth swept sparks down his chest, stiffening his loin as if he'd never kissed a woman before. He pulled her close, his body needing to feel her against him, and when she parted her lips, he accepted the invitation to explore.

Their tongues danced in circles, melding and caressing while her hands slipped around his waist and massaged the back of his spine. His body told him the kiss was a very bad idea. In a few short minutes he would have to descend to the restaurant and the stiff shaft tugging at his slacks was sure to make a fool of him. He didn't understand how a woman could continue to get him so hard, so fast, but as he brushed his hands up her waist and drove the kiss deeper, he lost the will to make sense of it.

Moans of pleasure filled his ears, like whispered promises of things to come.

Later.

After the dreaded, blasted dinner. As he pulled his lips away, he cursed the Tyndales for demanding a share of his time. He'd much rather they order room service and dine naked in the spa.

The ring of the phone tore him from the fantasy. He stepped back and reached for his cell as Trisha brushed the wetness from her lips.

"Are we late?" he asked, pulling the phone from his belt.

She glanced at her watch and shook her head.

WHILE LOGAN TOOK the call, Trisha stepped into the bathroom to touch up her makeup and comb her hair. Glancing at her image in the mirror, she silently thanked her blue dress for calling to her from the window at Saks Fifth Avenue that one spring day. Despite the steep price, she'd known she had to have it and the reaction she'd just received from Logan had been worth every cent.

His eyes had literally bulged from their sockets as

he stood there gaping at her, unable to utter a single word. Satisfaction curling her toes, she formed a wide grin, pressed a kiss to her fingers and tapped them against her dress—her beaded, blue best friend.

Nearly giddy, she finished up in the bathroom, took one last glance at her image and stepped out into the suite in time to hear Logan mutter something about chocolate mousse.

She raised an eyebrow as he snapped the phone shut and tossed it on the bar.

"Dinner's off," he said, his face fighting a wide grin.

"What happened?"

"It's awful, really. I shouldn't be so thrilled, but no one was hurt." He dropped the jacket from his shoulders, draped it over the chair and proceeded to loosen his tie.

"No one was hurt?"

"Apparently, there was a fire at Marc's Bonitas resort in Malibu. It wasn't bad. Started by a construction crew in a wing that was being remodeled." He kicked off his shoes. "I guess they contained it quickly and there weren't any injuries, but Marc and Corinne are leaving."

"They're leaving?"

The grin on his face won out when he snapped off his watch and set it next to the phone. "They need to survey the damage to find out how long construction will be delayed. We're on our own for the rest of the weekend."

Logan looked like a teenager who had just been handed the keys to his father's sports car. He could hardly contain his glee and as the situation sunk in, Trisha couldn't help the pleasure of her own.

He swept his eyes over her figure. "As much as I love that dress, you really need to take it off."

"What about dinner?"

He stepped to her, padding across the carpet in bare feet. Turning her back to his chest, he carefully released the clasp on her dress and slid the zipper down, trailing kisses over the skin it exposed.

"We're eating in. Room service will be here in a half hour." She clutched the front of her dress to keep it from falling to the floor. "Go change while I fill up the spa," he added.

She turned to face him, still trying to grasp the sudden change in plans. "The spa?"

His only answer was the sharp rise of his brow and sinister look of sex in his eyes. Dinner in the spa with Logan. The thought settled in, and when it did, her own face mirrored the delight on his.

"I'll be right back," she said, skipping to her room.

LOGAN ROLLED THE CART next to the spa where Trisha sat waiting, dropped his towel to the floor and stepped in the warm, churning water. The tub rested against a floor-to-ceiling window that provided a panoramic view of the ocean below. Polarized glass offered privacy while still allowing that feeling of being on the edge of the beach.

He had to hand it to Marc. The man definitely knew how to pick his hotels.

Logan slipped into one of the curved, molded seats

as Trisha settled over him, her slick, weightless body giving him all sorts of fun ideas. She laced her hands around his neck and kissed him lightly on his chin.

"So, what did you order?"

He cupped his hands to her breasts, enjoying the feel of the rushing water bringing life to the mounds in his hands. He fondled her nipples, allowing streams of bubbles to trickle through his fingers while he toyed with the pearl-like buds.

"Hmm, prawn cocktails on ice," he replied, trying to drum up interest in the meal. "I think there's some fruit in there, maybe a little bread and in exactly one hour, they're coming back with a couple fillets." He kissed the delicate skin under her ear. "This is just an appetizer."

"Fillets and what else?" she asked, tugging her lower lip against her teeth.

He chuckled. "I recall seeing chocolate mousse on the menu."

Her eyes lit with pleasure that he intended to turn into flames. Arching her back, she dipped under water, exposing the glistening breasts he'd been holding in his hands and while she wet her hair in the bubbles, he bent and took a bite.

She floated on the surface as he sucked at her breasts, sampling one for a moment before switching to the other. Her arms lapped at the water, pleasure blushed her cheeks, and with her hair gliding around her face, she looked like an angel swirling through the clouds.

Pulling her head from the water, she nestled back

on his lap, reaching under the waves to take hold of his erection.

"See what you do to me?" he asked, referring to the stiff, throbbing shaft in her hand.

A sleepy smile came over her face. Beads of water dripped down her cheeks, and when she raised her hips and slid his cock into her tight, slick core, she replied, "See what you do to me?"

She moved over him, allowing her hips to match the rhythm of the waves, and with each soothing stroke, his body responded. He ran his hands down her sleek, wet hair and sipped the dripping beads against her neck as her motion brought him higher. Their wet mouths clamped together, his tongue stroked against hers, and when he felt her nearing completion, he clutched his hands to her hips and pumped faster.

His mouth drinking her moans, his lungs inhaling her breath, he kept his eyes on hers, wanting to see the crush of surrender when the climax took her over. Her lids grew heavy, weighted by the sensation building between her legs, and when she closed her eyes, he knew the end was near.

"Look at me, baby," he whispered to her. "Keep your eyes on me."

Slowly, she raised her lids, allowing him access to the deepest corner of her soul, that naked spirit only her eyes could reveal. One by one, layers of control peeled away, every stroke taking her one step closer to the primal woman within, and the closer she got, the more vulnerable she became.

In this moment she was his, and he brought his

hands to her face, needing to study the emotion expressed in her gaze.

And what he saw stole his heart completely.

Raw, selfless beauty stared back at him. A giving of all she had and when the orgasm sent them sailing, he kept his eyes open and gave it all in return.

Joy, need, agony and delight churned in circles between them. Boundaries shattered. Barriers descended. And when the last burst of pleasure echoed through his veins, he pulled her head to his chest and held her in his arms.

Stroking her head in his hands, he watched the steam rise around them while her lips pressed wet kisses to his chest. And in the wake of glory, a swell of recognition swept over him.

He loved her.

God help him, he loved her.

He tightened the embrace, suddenly feeling as if he were holding on for dear life, as if the moment he let go, she'd slip out of his hands forever.

And the feeling left him terrified.

He hadn't wanted to ever relinquish control of his heart again, but it was gone, given to the woman in his arms, and at this point, there wasn't a damn thing he could do about it.

A silent curse escaped his lips, not as quietly as he'd hoped.

Trisha raised her head and smiled. "That was pretty amazing, wasn't it?"

He smiled back and kissed her on the lips. "Yes, amazing."

12

Daily Love Horoscopes for Pisces

You've been walking on clouds, but just make sure all that mist isn't blocking your view of the world around you. What you see may not be the reality that greets you when your feet hit the ground. Try not to let disappointment get in the way of what you want from life.

"DO YOU HAVE TO be so damn happy?" Bill asked.

Logan tried to wipe the smile from his face, but couldn't, at least, not all the way. Thanks to two blissful weeks with Trisha, a small corner of his mouth refused to straighten no matter how hard he tried to be sympathetic to Bill's situation.

It wasn't that he didn't feel for the man. It was never easy for a guy to propose, much less have the proposal turned down. But Logan had said it was a bad idea. If Bill had just listened to him, he and Adrienne would be shopping for baby clothes instead of chilling each other with frigid silence. And, more important, Bill would be off somewhere else, instead of stretched out on Logan's office couch like a patient undergoing therapy.

Logan snuck a peek at the clock on his credenza. It was after five o'clock and he feared Trisha might take off before he had a chance to ask her to dinner. Typically, they would have made plans by now, but thanks to a day packed with meetings and now Bill's impromptu psychotherapy session, Logan hadn't been able to touch base with her.

He took a sip of his coffee and winced at the thick, bitter taste. He should have known not to try the late-afternoon coffee from the break room, but he needed a boost of something strong to wake him up. Since he and Trisha had been back in town, neither of them had done much sleeping. It seemed they had months of twice-weekly chats to recreate, and it had become an unspoken quest to try to get through each and every one as quickly as possible.

Not that he was complaining. His love life had been stalled for years. It was about time he got a shot at happiness. It was unfortunate that it came at a time when Bill couldn't share in his joy.

Or wouldn't.

"Why do you have to be such a spoil sport?" he asked.

Bill's mouth cocked open in offense. "Have you forgotten my life is in the tank? Excuse me for not wanting your happiness shoved in my face."

Logan shot out a quick laugh. "For months, I had to listen to you whistling around the office while my love life was in the toilet. I never saw you sobering your smile for me."

"So, what's your point?"

"I'm the better man."

He figured the comment would take Bill's mind off his troubles, and Bill's choking look of shock proved him right.

"You're the better man?"

"My love life was shot for years. I never once rained on your parade." He looked at the date on his watch. "You've made it precisely two weeks. Proof that I'm the better man."

"Proof that you've had more practice at being miserable, that's all." Bill tucked his hands behind his head, the weary look of misery in his eyes shifting to the delight of the challenge. Bill loved a good debate, and Logan was pleased that his line of reasoning had worked. The sooner he cheered the man up, the sooner he could get out of here.

"I, on the other hand," Bill continued, "am completely unaccustomed to screwing up my life, so excuse me if I don't have your training."

"All you need to do is to apologize to Adrienne. Get a line of communication going."

Bill looked at him as if he were mad. "Since when does a man have to apologize for asking a woman to marry him?"

"Apologize for being a jerk when she turned you down." He held up a finger to stop Bill's impending objection. "And from what I understand, she didn't technically turn you down. That's just what your thick skull decided to hear."

"And what part of 'no' did I ignore?"

"The part where she said 'not now.' That doesn't mean never."

Bill snorted. "Come on. You know Adie. She's the procrastination queen. If we go by her schedule, we'll have a double wedding with our kid."

Logan took another sip of bitter coffee before setting it aside for good. His face still clenched from the taste, he replied, "I'm sure somewhere between now and the next twenty-five years, you'll find common ground. You two just need to talk."

"I've tried to talk. It makes everything worse." Bill shifted to his side and propped himself up on one elbow. "Get a load of the latest. She's actually thinking of having the baby at her folks' beach house out in Bodega."

Logan shrugged. "Well, not everyone has babies at the hospital these days."

"And what if something goes wrong? That's an hour away from the nearest hospital." Bill rolled onto his back, brushed his hands over his face and stared at the ceiling. "I could lose both of them before this even gets started."

"Well, jumping down Adrienne's throat isn't the way to change her mind."

"Who said I jumped down her throat?"

Logan gave him a hard stare.

"Well," Bill said, his voice tinged with defense. "You would, too, if you were in my shoes."

Logan tapped his fingers on the table, buying time while he collected his thoughts. He ought to get serious with Bill, not only for his own sake, but for the sake of the company. This tiff between him and Adrienne was beginning to create stress with everyone around them and while he'd hoped the two would work things out on their own, it didn't look as if that was going to happen in the near future.

"Bill, ever since you found out about this baby, you've been running a hundred miles an hour. You, of all people, know you can get way farther with sugar than you can a rubber mallet."

"I thought my marriage proposal was very sweet."

"And when she turned you down, you threw a fit and stormed out. Do you do that when a client disagrees with your ideas?"

"Of course not."

Logan took a breath and sighed. "Bill, come on. You're in advertising. Our entire business is based on the power of persuasion. You know how to get someone to buy into your ideas. For some reason, you've lost that talent with Adrienne." The look on Bill's face said Logan's words were sinking in. "Do you go into an ad meeting intending to beat the client into submission?"

His voice displaying reluctant agreement, Bill replied, "No."

"So why aren't you using your own inbred talent on Adrienne?"

Bill kept staring at the ceiling, flexing his jaw as he always did when his thoughts went into full swing. "You're right," he admitted. "I've been going about this all wrong." He pressed his hands to his face and spoke through his fingers. "Shit, I've been such a jerk. No wonder she keeps pushing back."

"You took the words right out of my mouth."

Bill released his hands and frowned. "Yeah, well just wait until your wife comes up pregnant someday. You won't be acting too rationally, either."

Logan chuckled. "No, if she's my wife, I would have lost my rationality long before any baby comes along."

TRISHA CHECKED her watch. It shocked her to see that it was already time to go home. At some point during the day, she would have expected Logan to pop his head in her office and ask what she was doing after work. He'd done so every day since they'd come back, but not today and she couldn't help but wonder why.

Granted, Logan and Bill had several meetings, but that had never stopped him before. He'd always found a moment to stop by to secure plans for that evening.

She tried to shrug off her disappointment. After all, she had to expect that eventually, Logan would have plans that conflicted with the two of them getting together. Certainly, she couldn't expect to spend each and every night with him, even though that had been the routine since they'd returned from their trip.

Well, maybe like her, he'd lost track of time. She wondered if she should stop by his office to say goodnight, give him one last opportunity to catch her before she went home.

Or would that look desperate?

She thought for a moment and shook her head. She should just leave. After all, she never made a habit of saying good-night before their trip to Cable Beach. Doing so now might send the wrong message. She should take off and catch up with him tomorrow. Besides, she knew men. At this point in a relationship, they were like frightened little puppies. One move too bold and they went skittering away. She didn't want to come off as clingy or presumptuous.

She pulled her purse from her desk and paused. What if he truly wanted to see her tonight and he'd lost track of time? He could think she wasn't interested or be put off by the fact that she left without saying a word. That was the last thing she wanted. But then again—

She exhaled a breath and plopped down in her chair. God, when had she gone from a confident woman to a starry-eyed teenager? The way she was acting, one would think she'd never dated a man before.

She smiled and closed her eyes, embarrassed over her own ridiculous thoughts. Truth was, if she had her way she'd move in with Logan and be done with the whole dating thing. She was already in love with him, had been even before their Caribbean weekend. She didn't need to wait to know he was the one she wanted to spend the rest of her life with. She already knew. These last two weeks had sealed it.

But instead, she was reduced to playing the dating game, trying to walk that line between possessiveness and indifference and she always hated that part of a budding relationship. So far, she had been spared even thinking about it. Logan had made every move before she even had a chance to contemplate when she'd see him again.

But today he hadn't, and not only did that leave her

with a dreaded pang of uncertainty, she was now stuck trying to calculate her next move.

Oh, what to do, what to do?

She supposed she didn't have to leave right now. She could hang for a while longer and see if he showed up.

Right. What are you going to do, Trisha, sit here all night? How moronic is that?

She glanced at the dozen long-stemmed roses that adorned her desk, Logan's Valentine's gift to her. Well, one of them, she chuckled. This was crazy, she thought, grabbing her purse and coat as she made her way out of the office. There was nothing presumptuous about saying good-night. And as for looking desperate, she would keep it casual without giving him the slightest sign that she expected anything more.

Because she didn't.

Really.

She stepped down the hall and stopped at Logan's doorway. He and Bill were talking and neither had seen her arrive. She raised her hand, intending to rap on the opened door when a comment gave her pause.

"Oh, don't tell me you're still on that I'm-never-getting-married kick. I thought things were going great between you and Trisha," Bill said.

She lowered her arm and took half a step back as the air trapped in her lungs.

"What does that have to do with anything?"

Bill shrugged. "I just thought when you found the right woman you'd want to settle down. I thought you wanted a family."

Logan sighed and shook his head. "Hasn't Adrienne taught you anything? You don't need marriage to have a family."

Bill chuckled out a warning. "Trisha isn't Adrienne."

"Well, the right woman for me will accept the fact that marriage is a long way off."

Trisha couldn't stop the low sound of surprise that crept from her throat and captured their attention. Logan's eyes turned to the door and widened at the sight, causing a rush of heat to flush her cheeks.

In a fit of despair and confusion, she stumbled over the words, "I—I just dropped in to say good night."

Her mouth ran dry. She didn't want to be here. She didn't want to have heard what she just heard and not only was she standing here feeling like a sordid eavesdropper, anger welled in her eyes, threatening to embarrass her further.

"I'll see you in the morning," she said, forcing a reluctant smile on her face as she turned and rushed to the lobby.

Pushing through the glass double doors, she stepped to the elevator and jabbed a finger at the button, praying that it would open and take her out of this situation.

What did that mean? *Marriage is a long way off.* Granted, she wasn't in a rush for commitment, but he'd made it sound as if they were years from anything serious.

Fire raged in her cheeks. What a fool she'd been, thinking their relationship was more than a convenient, nightly romp in the hay. She thought he'd cared more than that. He'd given her all kinds of signals telling her they were on to something that might last. Hell, half his clothes were at her apartment. He'd given her a key to his house, for heaven's sake. Things had been progressing between them.

But progressing to what, a life as his mistress?

She pressed the elevator button again, wishing the damn thing would hurry. She had to think about what she'd just heard, go over the last two weeks in her mind and figure out where she'd gone so colossally wrong.

And more importantly, what she should do now that she knew.

"Trisha."

The sound of Logan's voice escalated her nerves. She couldn't deal with him right now. She needed time to think this through, but obviously that wasn't going to be an option. Reluctantly she turned to see him pass through the double doors, his face wrought with concern and laced with a hint of fear.

"I…" he started, obviously not knowing where to go from there, and she certainly didn't, either.

Being angry didn't seem appropriate. Though that was the overriding emotion at the moment, she wasn't sure she had the right to be mad. After all, they'd only been dating two weeks. Discussing marriage at this point seemed premature, but she couldn't hide the crush of knowing that he'd placed it on the shelf indefinitely.

The air turned thick with discomfort. She shouldn't have been listening in on the conversation, and for that, she was truly sorry. But she couldn't get over the words she heard, and as much as she wanted to brush it off, the anger and hurt wouldn't subside.

She desperately wanted the elevator doors to open and take her away, but at this point, even an elevator couldn't relieve them from the spot they'd just been put in. They were trapped, forced to discuss a matter that stood like a brick wall between them.

She tilted her head toward his office and forced herself to speak. "That in there—was that just guy talk or is that how you really feel?"

He brushed a hand through his hair. "Trisha," he started again, pausing for a moment before he went on. "I'm not afraid of commitment. Please don't think that."

"It didn't sound that way to me."

"I'd like to settle down someday. I want a family of my own. But..." His shoulders fell in defeat. "No, marriage isn't something I'm going to jump into anytime soon."

She bit her lip and stiffened her chin, trying to hide the devastation of his words. Swallowing hard to clear her throat, she replied, "I appreciate your honesty."

He reached out an arm and touched her cheek. "Honey, it doesn't change the way I feel about you."

"And how is that, exactly?"

"I love you."

The elevator doors opened, but her legs wouldn't move. He'd said the words she'd dreamed of hearing, expressed the same affection she held for him, but somehow, instead of making her feel better, it made everything worse.

"You *love* me?" She didn't expect the question to be loaded with such anger.

The sheepish smile on Logan's face faded. "Trisha, I'd like to share my life with you."

"As what, your permanent mistress?"

His mouth dropped as if he were about to speak, but for a long moment, nothing came out. Slowly he shook his head. "I won't be pushed into marriage again."

She studied the conviction in his gaze. Up until now she hadn't realized how thoroughly his ex-wife had destroyed him. Virginia had literally ruined him for any woman who came along after her. God, he really must have loved her, and the thought churned her emotions in circles of rage, devastation and bitter jealousy.

"You love me, but you don't trust me."

"What?"

"You don't trust that I love you and not your company."

"No," he replied, but the defensiveness in his tone told her she'd nailed the issue.

"Yes. Trust, Logan, remember? It was the one thing Pisces needed more than love and it's the one thing you won't give me."

His jaw dropped, but she really didn't need an answer. It was written all over his face. He would take a stab at love again, but he would never open up fully, as he had with Virginia. His shield would always be raised, ready for the day Trisha dropped the bomb, which he would forever expect her to do.

"I do trust you," he finally said.

"No, you don't. As long as I work here, you'll always wonder if I'm just another Virginia, out to take your business."

"Oh, Trisha, come on. That's not what this is about."

"It's exactly what this is about." The elevator had come and gone, so she punched the button again.

"Trisha, lots of people don't rush into marriage."

She turned to face him, taking a step closer so he could see the certainty in her eyes. "I know that, but this isn't about taking our time. You aren't against commitment, you said it yourself. Your issue's with trust. As long as you aren't married, no woman can ruin you completely. Isn't that it?"

"No," he attempted, but she saw through the false denial.

"Fine. Kid yourself, but you aren't kidding me." She took another step toward him, her chin nearly touching his chest. Looking deeply into his eyes, she asserted, "All I ever wanted was you, Logan. I don't want your company. I thought you knew that about me."

"I do."

She shook her head. "No. Not deep down in your heart."

He stared into her eyes until the elevator bell broke the silence. She turned and stepped toward the doors. "I quit. I'll clear out my things tomorrow."

Logan rushed up behind her as she stepped inside. "You can't be serious."

"As long as I work for this agency, you'll never believe that it's you I want."

He stood for a moment, holding the door with his hand, his eyes wide with shock, until slowly they darkened. "So that's it. Marry you or you'll leave?"

Now she was the one shocked. "What?"

"Is this an ultimatum? Marriage or nothing?"

She folded her arms over her chest. "You didn't hear a word I said, did you?"

He responded with a nod. "Oh, I heard you, all right. I marry you or it's over."

She opened her mouth to object, but stopped.

Is that what she'd said?

No, it wasn't. She shook her head, trying to convince herself that he'd simply minced her words. "I'm not asking for a proposal."

"Then what are you asking for?" The anger in his eyes was clearly evident now.

"I—I'm asking you to trust me."

"And the only way to prove that is marriage. Is that it?"

She didn't like the way he phrased it, but she couldn't come up with anything better. Was that truly what she had said? In a sense, yes, but it seemed harsh when spoken like that. But no matter how blunt, it was true.

Or was it?

She couldn't think clearly. This was all happening too fast. They shouldn't be issuing ultimatums. That wasn't what this was about and she wanted to back down, to shake her head and say no, but the words wouldn't come to her lips.

This was a crossroads, the direction she chose now setting the path for the rest of their relationship. And pretending marriage didn't matter wasn't an option. It did matter. Not only because she believed in the institution, but because without it, she would never feel that Logan was fully hers. She would always be second fiddle to Virginia Matthews, the one and only woman he would have ever truly trusted.

Unable to think straight, she simply stood and stared.

Logan released his hand from the door and took a step back, his eyes filled with deep betrayal.

"Then go," he said as the elevator doors closed between them.

13

LOGAN LOOKED OUT over the San Francisco skyline, trying to figure out how his life had gone from heaven to hell in a matter of five minutes. Three days ago, he had woken up in the arms of the woman he loved. Today, he'd awakened to a cold, empty house, all traces of her gone except for the key she'd left on his counter and the scent of lavender still lingering on his sheets.

He'd instructed his housekeeper to get rid of his bedding, pillows and all, not explaining that it was simply too painful having it around. The memories were hard enough.

She'd looked at him as if he'd lost his mind.

No argument there.

From the moment he'd discovered Trisha Bain was Scorpio, his sensibility had taken leave. He'd dodged all the warning flags and hopped in the deep end all over again, thinking this time he could stay above water. He'd wanted to believe the warnings were just illusions, hallucinations created by a painful past that wouldn't let go.

Until one popped up that was too big to ignore.

Marriage or nothing.

Damn it, Virginia had done the very same thing, issued that same ultimatum that had led him to the greatest mistake of his life. Back then, he would have done anything to keep her. Marriage was a no-brainer, and he had responded with a resounding "I do." Hell, even this time his heart had pleaded with him to do whatever it took to keep Trisha by his side, even if that meant going down the aisle again.

But there was a saying about fools doing the same thing and expecting a different result. Boy, wasn't that the truth? He'd fallen in love with Trisha, ignored all the similarities between her and Virginia and expected something new.

Which made him a colossal fool.

He trailed his eyes over the damp, gray skyline. The fog settled over the bay, casting gloom over the murky city streets. A couple of tourists shuffled down Market Street, shivering in their shorts and tanks. The tourists were easy to spot in San Francisco. They were the ones who expected California to welcome them with bright, sunny days. But it was the locals who knew that sunshine in San Francisco could turn to frigid cold before you could say Alcatraz and you'd better come prepared.

"So, she's really gone."

Logan turned to see Bill standing in the doorway. "Hmm?" he asked.

"Trisha. Her office is cleared out."

He stepped from the window and took a seat at his desk, his legs suddenly tired from the weight in his chest.

"Yes, she must have come in over the weekend."

Though he wasn't sure when. He'd spent long hours here since she'd left Friday afternoon, purposely avoiding his home. He hadn't wanted to step into his bedroom and catch another sight of her robe draped casually over his chair. He hadn't wanted to stare at it, as if it held the soul of his lost love, or to fight the urge to touch it. And when he'd come home Sunday, it was gone, along with all her other things. The clothes he'd left at her house had been carefully hung in his closet and all her possessions had been removed, replaced by that one silver key.

He wasn't certain which was worse, fighting the instinct to clutch her things, or coming home and finding them gone.

"So, that's it," Bill said, taking a seat at his desk. "You're just going to let her leave."

"I don't want to talk about it."

Bill ignored the statement and went on. "She's not another Virginia. How many times do I have to tell you that?"

"We'll just have to see what agency she pops up at and how many accounts she tries to steal away."

Just the thought left him sick to his stomach. He didn't want to believe Trisha would really do it, but history was on the path of repeating itself. He had to accept what his future might hold.

Bill shook his head. "She's not going to do that."

"Still, if she tries, I'll be one step ahead of her." He rested his elbows on the desk and laced his fingers together. "I had a chat with Nick Coulter this morning. He's very interested in the VP position."

Bill's mouth dropped open. "You're going to replace her, just like that?"

"I need to fill the position before things start falling by the wayside." Another mistake he'd made with Virginia that he wouldn't repeat.

"Look, I'm getting together with Adie tomorrow night. We're going to talk. Let me find out what's going on with Trisha before you go making any moves."

Logan shook his head. "Concentrate on your own problems. I've got mine under control. Besides," he said, checking his watch. "I'm meeting with Nick in an hour and I've got to run by Human Resources first. If all goes well, I'll have my new VP before the day is out."

"This is a big mistake."

No, falling in love with Trisha had been a big mistake, and the quicker Logan moved on, the quicker he could put her in the past and get back to life as it was. Miserable as that might be.

TRISHA STOOD in the center of her vast glass-walled office. Or at least, what would be her office if all went well.

"What do you think?"

She turned and glanced at her mother. "It's huge."

Monica Bain chuckled, her blue eyes mixed with delight and tender sorrow. "You sure this is what you want?"

"Mom, this is the opportunity of a lifetime," she replied, as much to convince herself as well as her mother. "Head of marketing for Sunwest Bank? Are you sure the board will go along with it?"

"Ironically, you were the first person I'd had in mind

when the position opened. I just never dreamed you'd want to leave the Moore agency."

Monica stood close to her daughter and ran a hand over her hair. The touch took Trisha back to when her mother would brush her hair and show her how to twirl it into a French twist. She missed those simple days.

"Well, I don't have much practice managing staff."

"That's what training is for. The important thing is your agency experience. You'll be the liaison for our outside marketing firms. We've been looking for someone with your contract experience and understanding of what goes on at the other end. The rest will be easy."

Trisha ran her hand over the glossy cherrywood desk. The thought of taking a high position in such a large corporation bordered on surreal. She almost had to pinch herself to believe it was true. It was just a shame the ache in her heart dampened her joy.

"He didn't call?" Monica asked.

She looked at her mother, tears threatening to well in her eyes, not just over Logan, but the fact that her mom always seemed so in tune to her thoughts.

"No, he's not going to call."

"And you don't think this is something you two could work out if you talked? You really seemed to care for each other."

She forced out a bitter laugh. "All he cares about is protecting his company." And the fact that he thought she wanted it was insulting enough. Crawling back to him at this point was out of the question. "No," she added, "The Moore Agency is his one and only love and I wish them both a very happy life together."

"From what you told me, he's been hurt. He could just need some patience." Monica brushed a finger over Trisha's cheek. "I know how proud you can be at times."

Trisha widened her eyes, not believing her ears. "Mom, you're the one who told me never to settle for less than what I wanted. You're the one who said I should never enter a relationship thinking I can change a man."

Monica nodded and sheepishly smiled. "Yes, I suppose I did. But your relationship was a budding one. Maybe with a little more time, he'll come around. People aren't completely unchangeable, you know."

Now Trisha knew her mother had gone mad. "What am I supposed to do, waste the best years of my life on a man who doesn't trust me? What kind of relationship is that?"

Monica shrugged her shoulders. "If you're certain he won't come around…"

"No," she said with a renewed sense of resolve. "I did exactly what I should have done. I got out while I had the chance." She turned to the door and glanced at the vast sea of cubicles and offices. "Besides, I'll bet this place is crawling with eligible bachelors."

Monica chuckled. "Well, I don't know if bankers are your style, but there's probably one or two who might catch your eye."

Trisha smiled, feeling refreshed for the slew of interviews that awaited her. She looked at her watch. "Almost time for my first meeting."

Monica patted a hand on her shoulder. "Let's go."

As they stepped out the door, Trisha stopped and eyed her mother. "You did that on purpose."

"Did what?"

"Played devil's advocate to cheer me up."

Monica frowned and led her down the hall. "I did no such thing."

BILL STARED AT Adrienne's door, his hand held up in a fist poised to knock, but before he did, he took one long, calming breath. Though he knew his and Adrienne's futures were sealed together, he couldn't shake the feeling that this meeting was his last chance at resolving their fate. Like a client who was ready to pull the plug, this was his last pitch to try to land the account.

And he'd prepared as such. Logan's words had made sense. He'd been doing this all wrong, firing off shots and demanding his way like a spoiled child fighting for the last bag of chips. And thanks to Logan's analogy, Bill had decided to approach this meeting as he had every other campaign he'd tried to win. He'd strategized, studied the client's needs and came up with the ideas he needed to land the love of his life.

And as if this were his very first sales pitch, he was at the door of his client's office, shaking with nerves. Though he knew in his heart, he'd have plenty of chances with Adrienne, he couldn't shake the gravity of this moment. He really wanted this to work, because if it didn't, he wasn't sure what else to do.

Grasping another breath of air, he held it in and rapped on the door, seconds seeming like hours as he waited for her to greet him. He heard footsteps, the sound of soft music, followed by the click of the dead bolt, then, in front of him, stood Adrienne, her face tired and worn.

Regret swept over him when he realized that he was responsible for the haggard look in her dark sage eyes. They'd been battling for weeks, and at this moment, with the soft wisps of golden strands framing her weary face, he wished he could take it all back.

He bent and kissed her forehead. "Hi, sweetheart."

Her smile was brief as she backed from the doorway and padded across the floor to take a seat on the couch. "I'm a little worn out today," she said. "There's a beer in the fridge if you'd like one."

He closed the door behind him. "No, thanks." Following her to the couch, he took a seat next to her. For no other reason than to ease his nerves, he reached out and tucked a loose strand of hair behind her ear. "How are you feeling?"

She took in a breath and sighed. "Fat and exhausted."

"I'm sorry, hon. Can I do something for you?"

Her expression turned suspicious. "What's up your sleeve, Bill?"

He figured she wouldn't make this easy, but he guessed he deserved it. He hadn't been the greatest guy lately.

"An apology," he said.

Rather than easing the wary look in her eyes, his comment just caused them to narrow farther.

"For what?" she asked.

A low chuckle formed in his chest and escaped his lips. "How much time do we have?"

She studied him for a moment, her gradual look of

ease giving him hope. She trailed her gaze down his chest and back to his face, her shoulders gently relaxing as she realized he hadn't come to continue the war. He was slowly getting his Adie back and if he kept playing his cards right, he'd keep her where he wanted for good.

Pinching her chin between his thumb and forefinger, he kissed her lips. "I'm sorry for being a jerk. I'm sorry for pressuring you, and not listening to you, and making demands and stomping my feet and yelling—"

She pressed a finger to his mouth. "I think that's a good enough start."

The tension eased at the base of his neck. "I have a better start," he said. "Where's the ring I bought you?"

The shield of defense returned to her eyes, causing him to press another kiss to her lips. "Relax, honey," he whispered. "It's not what you think."

She bit her lower lip and eyed him with suspicion, then finally replied, "It's in my jewelry box."

She began to rise from the couch but he tapped a hand to her shoulder. "I know where it is. Just sit."

He crossed to her bedroom and took the decorated box from her closet. Lifting the lid, he pulled out the ring, stashed the box back on the shelf and returned to the living room.

He handed her the ring. "Hold this."

Reluctantly, she took the diamond in her hand as he reached into his pocket and pulled out a sparkling gold chain. He threaded the chain through the ring and bent to clasp it around her neck. Still looking confused, Adrienne allowed him to place the chain around her neck, her eyes displaying caution, but beginning to soften with relief.

"Keep this near your heart," he said. "And when we feel the time is right, we'll talk about putting it on your finger." He kissed her lips. "How does that sound?"

She moved a shaky hand to her chest and pressed the ring to her palm as her eyes grew glassy with tears. "That sounds perfect," she said, her voice cracked with emotion.

"No more battles. From now on, you handle the pregnancy as you see fit and I'll support whatever decisions you make."

"Really?" Her voice was as soft as a reluctant child's.

He smiled and nodded, the gleam in her gaze filling him with joy.

"You know," she said. "It's our baby. Everything doesn't have to be my way, either."

"I think if I do more listening and less talking, we'll find a way to compromise." He tapped a finger to the ring resting against her chest. "Like this."

She raised her hand and covered his. "Like this."

A long sigh rushed from her lungs as she wrapped her arms around him and squeezed tight until the air trapped in his chest. Her tears wetting his cheek, she whispered to his ear, "I love you, Bill."

And he squeezed her back, being careful not to clutch too tightly, though the three blissful words she'd just spoken made it difficult.

She loved him. She finally admitted she loved him. And in the soft light of the evening, he realized that deep down it was something he already knew.

"I'm sorry, honey."

She pulled back and sniffed, wiping a tear from her

cheek. "So am I. It's just that…between you and my family—"

He cupped her face in his hands. "That's over. Like I said, you handle the pregnancy as you see fit. If you want to have the baby at the beach, that's okay with me." He decided against telling her he'd already arranged for a paramedic friend to stand on call.

"Actually, I'm having it at U.C. San Francisco."

He checked her face to see if she was joking. "You are?"

She nodded. "I'm not crazy about the beach house idea, either, and I figured the last thing I needed was you strung out on nerves through the delivery."

Every muscle in his body relaxed, and up until now, he hadn't realized how important that had been to him.

"That's really what you want?" he asked.

Her smile was warm and genuine. "Yes. In fact, I've got an appointment to tour the maternity ward next week. Can you come?"

"I wouldn't miss it." He kissed her again, the soft feel of her skin against his lips reminding him that it had been a long time since he'd held her in his arms and he quickly wanted more.

As if she'd read his mind, she stood and took his hand. "I've missed you," she said, her eyes lit with a fire he hadn't seen in weeks.

He had his Adie back. She loved him. And as he rose and followed her to her room, his world clicked into place.

The two tore off clothing like sex-starved teenagers rushing against the clock, kicking off shoes and shrugging off shirts, until they bounded for the bed and the love they'd been denied.

Bill pulled her against him and placed a hand on her abdomen, taking the moment to enjoy the comfort of her body against his. "You feel it kick yet?"

She chuckled. "Once, I thought I did, but I think it was just lunch disagreeing with me."

He shimmied down the bed and pressed an ear to her stomach. "I can hear it."

"No you can't. It's too soon."

He shifted to the other ear so he could watch her face. "You're right. Sounds like salad."

Her laugh rumbled against his ear, filling his heart with so much pleasure, he thought it might burst. And the sexy look in her eye promised more to come.

She reached out her hands and pulled him over her, pressing warm kisses to his chin. "I've missed you."

"I've missed you, too," he said, shifting his stiff cock to her entrance as proof.

She parted her legs in welcome and he responded by slowly sliding in, burying his shaft inside the woman he loved, relishing every inch of her body under and around him. This was the place he belonged, in this bed, with this woman, with their child resting peacefully between them.

"I love you, Adie," he said as he gently stroked inside her, holding his motion steady to stretch out the moment for as long as his anxious cock would allow.

A sleepy fire burned in her eyes, telling him she wouldn't need much time, either. "I love you, too," she said, then moaned as pure satisfaction overcame her face.

Together, they moved, stroking in rhythm as the sensation crested, sweeping higher and higher until Bill wasn't sure he could go on. And just as he feared his climax might come too soon, Adrienne's chest heaved as she shattered around him. Her legs clamped tightly around his calves, her fingers dug into his chest and as her core pulsed against his shaft, he cried out in release.

The orgasm took control of his motion, jerking and buckling until weeks of pent-up desire and frustration drained away to warm, temperate relaxation. Afraid to collapse on her chest, he quickly fell to the side and pulled her body against his.

"I guess we'll have to be quieter when the baby comes," he said, kissing her glistening forehead. "It'll be a little strange making love with a crib in the corner of the room."

She pressed a kiss to his lips, dropped her head against the pillow and began fondly touching his hair. "Actually, I've been thinking about that, too."

"Pray tell."

"Well…" She clamped her lip between her teeth. "What would you think about us getting a place together? Somewhere that would be ours, with more than one bedroom and maybe…a garage?"

Something about the way she said "garage" grabbed his attention. "Sounds like you're rethinking the apartment?"

"It's just that I have to park down on the street and this isn't the greatest neighborhood. And Robin was telling me what a pain it is to lug around a baby when you've got groceries and things, and without a garage,

I can't leave the baby in the car while I carry in groceries and I don't want to leave the baby upstairs while I'm downstairs and—"

"Are you saying you need another pair of hands?"

She flashed a reluctant smile. "Not exactly. What I really want is our baby to come home to its mommy and daddy."

He winked. "And another pair of hands wouldn't hurt."

"And a place with a garage would be great." She pushed him onto his back and mounted him, her sparkling ring dangling their promise between them. "And a nursery down the hall, so you can scream like you will very shortly." She flicked an eyebrow just in case he hadn't caught her meaning. Not that she had to. A certain part of his body heard her loud and clear.

He clasped a hand around the back of her neck and pulled her mouth to his. "It all sounds wonderful, honey."

And in her smile, he saw she agreed.

14

"LOGAN, NICK COULTER IS on line one. He has a few questions about the offer."

"Thanks, Kelly." Logan rose from his conference table, intentionally avoiding eye contact with Bill. He didn't want to see the look on his face, but when he stepped to his desk, he could feel Bill's gaze burning a hole in his back even before the man spoke.

"You can't be serious."

Reluctantly he turned, Bill's shocking look of disgust exactly what he'd expected.

"I have an opening I need to fill."

"You haven't even called her, have you?"

If picking up the phone and dialing five of the seven numbers counted, he'd called Trisha at least a dozen times. But actually following through, allowing the phone to ring, allowing her to answer so he could say the words he knew she ought to hear—no, he hadn't been able to do it.

Not that the urge hadn't consumed him for the past ten days. Since Bill had come back with the news of her new job, Logan hadn't been able to concentrate on anything else, including the offer he'd made to Nick

Coulter. It was no surprise that Nick was calling with questions. It was probably the most poorly written job offer Logan had ever written, so vague even he wasn't sure exactly what he was offering.

He knew his subconscious was trying to sabotage the deal and he knew exactly why. He wanted Trisha back. The problem was, every time he picked up the phone to call her, he had no idea what to say exactly.

I'm sorry? I was completely wrong about you? I should have trusted you from the beginning?

Bill would tell him any of those would be a fine start, but every time Logan imagined her response, it wasn't good. Truth was he didn't deserve Trisha's forgiveness. He deserved to spend the rest of his life alone, and maybe in some strange way, he was punishing himself for being such a stupid fool.

He glanced at Bill, still sitting with his mouth agape and a disgusted frown on his face as he waited for an answer.

"I—" he started, not sure where to go from there.

Bill closed his mouth, folded his arms across his chest and stared him down, forcing Logan to pick the first thing that popped into his head.

"Well, she hasn't exactly called me, either, you know."

The moment the words slipped out, he realized how ridiculous he sounded and Bill spared no effort in underscoring that notion.

"Oh, that's really mature."

"Goddamn it, Bill, I don't know what to say, all right? Happy?" He leaned over and pressed his palms on the desk, diverting his eyes from the blinking light on his phone. "I screwed up. I treated her horribly. Every step of the way, I thought the worst, and now she's gone and it's my own damn fault."

"Sounds to me like you know exactly what to say."

"Yeah, and none of that will bring her back. You said it yourself. She looked happy, more relaxed than you've seen her in months. She's got a big cushy job at a company that can offer her more than I ever could."

"Oh, break out the violins. Would you listen to yourself? You're pathetic. In fact," he chuckled, "I can't even believe I actually work for you right now." When Logan didn't respond, Bill huffed and calmed his tone. "Look, you gave me some sage advice last week. Now let me ask you the same question. Do you treat your clients like this? Do you go into a sales pitch with your shoulders slumped, expecting to fail?"

He stood for a moment, letting Bill's words take hold. No, he'd never had a defeatist attitude when it came to work, because when it came to business, the stakes were never this high. He could handle losing clients. It happened every day. But he couldn't handle losing Trisha, and if he cut through all the garbage he kept feeding himself, he knew that was the truth lying underneath it all.

He couldn't handle discovering that he'd lost Trisha for good.

As long as he avoided her, he wouldn't have to face the finality of their situation. As long as he left things unsaid, he would never have to hear her rejection.

Everything that had been going through his mind

was just a mental ploy to skate the real issue. It was easier to assume she wouldn't take him back than to know it as a fact. He could convince himself that he didn't deserve her or that she was better off without him. But he couldn't stand up and risk taking that slap in the face he so greatly feared.

When it came to Virginia, a part of him could blame her. She was the villain in that relationship. But he didn't have that crutch when it came to Trisha. If he lost her, too, he'd have no one to blame but himself and it was that fact that would surely break him for good.

He winced, not wanting to humiliate himself with the truth in front of Bill, but he knew it was time to get real.

"What if it's too late?"

"It's not going to be too late."

He stared at the phone, the blinking light screaming in his eyes, demanding his attention.

Demanding he make a decision.

It's not going to be too late. Bill's words repeated in his mind, the soft assuredness in his tone echoing in his ears.

But could he trust those words? And, more important, did he have a choice but to believe them?

Reaching for the phone, he pressed a finger to the intercom. "Kelly, please tell Nick I'll have to call him back."

TRISHA SNAPPED THE LID on her laptop, tucked it in the case then carried it out of her office with her travel bag.

"Oh, just leave those. The driver will come take them," said Inga, her secretary.

She paused for a moment, still trying to get used to the services provided to bank executives—services that included a personal assistant and a driver to take her to the airport. Inga was continually snipping at her for making her own appointments and travel arrangements and it had become a joke between the two that Inga's job entailed breaking in the new executive.

She set the bags next to her door. "Okay, thanks."

"Mrs. Bain is just getting out of her meeting. I'll ring when she's ready to go."

"Great," Trisha replied, stepping back into her office.

Taking a seat at her desk, she checked her watch, anxious to get on the road. The new job wouldn't involve much travel after this initial visit to the bank's parent corporation, but Trisha looked forward to getting out of town for a few days. It had been over a week since she announced her new job to Bill and Adrienne, which meant it had been that long since Logan knew.

She'd thought the news would have brought him around, proving that she wasn't another Virginia out to steal his business. But days had passed without a peep from Logan and her disappointment had worn down to surrender. Each day, she'd come home, her eyes darting to the answering machine the moment she opened the door, and each day the machine greeted her with a red digital zero. She'd jumped every time the phone rang, perked every time she heard footsteps up the stairs, and each time it wasn't Logan, her heart tore a little further.

It was time to get out of town.

She needed the change of pace and some time alone with her mother would help ease the pain of her loss.

Logan never called, and she'd finally come to the conclusion that the relationship was over. It was time to move on, to take solace in the fact that she hadn't wasted years hoping for something that would never be.

The trip would be good for her, an opportunity to get out of the confines of her empty home, look to her future and start building a new life and a new career.

"Are these your bags, Ms. Bain?"

A man in a black suit stood in her doorway, pointing to her laptop and luggage.

"Yes."

"I'm parked in front whenever you're ready."

She nodded and followed the driver out just as her mother approached.

"Ready?"

Before Trisha could answer, Inga interrupted. "There's a Logan Moore here to see you. I told him you were on your way out, but he said it's important."

Shock widened her eyes as she turned to her mother.

"Send him up," Monica replied.

"But—"

"We've got a few minutes. I'm going to make a quick call and I'll meet you at the car."

She zipped off before Trisha could object.

Stepping back to her office, she tried hard to stifle her hope. If Logan had come wanting her back, he would have done it days ago, when news of her job at the bank proved once and for all she hadn't been after his agency. He'd probably come to discuss something regarding Tyndale and given the circumstances, felt he should do it in person.

She clenched her hands together, wondering what he wanted and hoping the meeting would be brief. She was just starting the process of healing and she didn't need a meeting with Logan to tear open fresh wounds.

"Hey."

The sound of his caramel-smooth voice caused her to jump and turn to the door, and a swell of emotion swept up her throat. Though he looked polished as always, his face showed otherwise. The tired lines tautened his cheeks, faint bags hung under his eyes and his shoulders had slumped from their usual confident stance.

She wondered if she looked as tired, and in a move of defense, she straightened and jutted her chin.

"I was on my way out. What can I do for you?"

His dark eyes lowered at her terse words, and a pang of regret threatened to crumble her composure. She hadn't meant to sound cruel. She only wanted Logan to speak his business and leave before every thread holding her together snapped from the weight of his presence.

"We need to talk," he said, stepping into the office.

"I don't have much time. If this is about Tyndale, I could call you—"

"This isn't about Tyndale. We need to talk about us." He moved closer and she swallowed hard, darting her eyes away from the gaze that always managed to melt her insides. "I have a lot to apologize for, the foremost being I should have trusted you from the start."

She looked up to see dark eyes laced with sorrow and regret, and for what seemed like a long moment, he just stood and stared, maybe trying to read her expression, maybe expecting her to have some sort of reaction. But at the moment, her thoughts were too confused to process anything. She'd expected this a week ago, ached for it, gone to sleep every night a little more disappointed that another day had passed without it.

And now he'd come after she'd finally rid herself of expectations, hopes and dreams. She wasn't sure what he wanted from her, and in all honesty, she wasn't even sure how she felt.

"Honey," he said, the endearment bringing a sour pang to her chest. "I've made a mistake. Things never should have come to this."

Reaching out, he took her hand, but she pulled it back, not ready for the intimacy of his touch. Her thoughts had waged battle, her hopeful side armed to fill her heart with joy, but the other side angry that she'd had to go through so much to prove her love.

The angry side won.

"And you've just now come around to this revelation?" she heard herself ask. She didn't recognize her scorned, bitter voice, the tone causing her to realize just how deep the wounds had gone.

He reached toward her, stopping short of clasping her shoulders, choosing to brush his hand over his face instead. "Trisha, I want us to start over. I want you back." Taking a small step closer, he hovered near her, his fresh, masculine scent clouding her thoughts, his broad form crumbling her nerves. She wanted him back, too, but under what circumstances? How much could he really give?

"I was wrong, Trisha. I was wrong about everything." Tilting his head to meet her gaze, he urged, "Please forgive me."

Her heart pressed her to rush to his arms, to pull him close and tell him how much she loved him, but something gave her pause—a tiny voice in her head that whispered words she couldn't quite hear. This didn't feel right, and when he pulled a gold ring from his pocket, the problem stood squarely in front of them.

"I'm in love with you," he said, "and I want you in my life—fully."

She spoke to the ring in his hand. "I wasn't asking for marriage. That's not what this is about."

"Yes, it is. I want to prove to you that I trust you in the only way I can."

She took a step back, needing to distance herself from what she wanted and what was right. And this regret-filled marriage proposal wasn't right. He shouldn't have to prove himself with a ring, just as she shouldn't have had to prove herself by taking the job at the bank.

"I need to think," she said.

He went to her, clasped a hand to her forearm, his eyes desperate from the notion that his efforts might be failing. "Virginia took everything I wanted from life. You can give it all back. I want it back, baby." Dropping the ring in his pocket, he clutched her other arm and held her tight. "Don't make me lose it all over again."

"What am I, just a replacement for the woman you loved?"

His eyes darkened. "That woman never deserved my love. And she never deserved the power I gave her to destroy my future with you." He brushed a hand over her cheek, the warmth of his touch bringing an ache to her tattered nerves. "What Virginia and I had wasn't love. You showed me that. You showed me what real love is supposed to be. I'd just been too broken to see it. The only thing I had for Virginia was hurt and regret and once I let that go, she ceased to exist."

She couldn't deny the sincerity in his eyes and the sweet sensation of his touch made her yearn to believe his words.

"I don't deserve you," he said, "but if you'll give me one more chance, I'll show you how much you mean to me."

The wall around her heart began to crumble. He'd said what she wanted to hear, that Virginia was a woman he'd truly put in the past, and his admission dissolved her fears and opened her mind to the future they could share—the future she'd always dreamed of.

Holding her face in his hands, he spoke closely to her lips. "Let's start over. Let's do this right."

"I'm sorry, Ms. Bain. Mrs. Bain is waiting in the limo. You need to leave now or you'll miss your plane."

Trisha glanced over his shoulder to see Inga standing in the threshold. "I've got to go."

"Please don't. Come back to the agency."

She looked into his eyes, the desire and urgency in them nearly causing her to go along, but she had an obligation to her new job and her mother. "I can't. I have to go."

"No, you don't," he said. "Come back with me where you belong."

She opened her mouth, nearly spilling words of acceptance. In a heartbeat, she could have dropped everything, taken his hand and ran off with him in the sunset, but her mother had gone through a lot to get her this position. She couldn't just walk away from it now.

"I'm sorry," Inga said. "You really need to get to the limo."

Pulling away, Trisha stepped to the door. "I have to go."

Logan turned. "Trisha, please."

"I have to go. I'll call you when I get to Chicago."

And with that, she crossed the floor and made her way downstairs, leaving Logan standing in her office. Her limbs shook, the uncertainty of her choice leaving her more confused than before. She did want him back and she wanted him now. She'd wanted to throw herself into his arms and taste those lips she thought she'd never kiss again. But stepping through the lobby, she mentally confirmed her obligations. Like it or not, she'd taken a new job, one she felt she would truly enjoy. And if Logan truly loved her, he would wait until she had a chance to sort things out.

The driver stood by the limo door and she ducked inside, taking a seat next to her mother.

"So, what did Logan want?" Monica asked as they pulled away from the curb.

"He asked me to marry him."

She looked down to Trisha's hand. "I don't see a ring on your finger."

"I couldn't accept it. Not yet."

Monica stared at her with that knowing look. "I thought you loved him."

Trisha's frustration came through in her voice. "I do and he said everything I'd hoped he'd say. But I can't ignore all that's happened recently. I've got a new job with new responsibilities. We're on our way to Chicago. Now was not the time to waltz in with a marriage proposal and expect me to just waltz out with him."

Monica took her hand and held it tight. "Trisha, would you like to know the first rule of business?"

She looked to her mother and nodded, needing all the help she could get.

"First rule of business is family comes first."

LOGAN FLICKED ON the lights to his den, glancing at the clock for the fourth time in five minutes. After leaving Trisha, he'd returned to the office to find an e-mail from her asking him to meet her at LoveSigns at eight o'clock. Since then, the moments hadn't ticked by fast enough and nervous jitters took over his hands as the clock neared eight. Her note said nothing else and she hadn't answered his calls. The wait was killing him, and with five minutes left to go, he opted to sign on so he could be there the moment she arrived.

Clicking in to the site, his heart jumped a beat when he saw that she'd already logged on. Maybe she was as anxious as he and he wondered if that was good or bad.

Raising his hands to the keyboard, he paused, unsure what he should say or who should start, but he couldn't wait any longer. He typed in the words, "Hey, beauti-ful," and clicked Send.

"Hey," the screen read back. After a moment, more words popped up. "You said something about starting over. I think I'd like that."

A quick jolt sped up his pulse. "I'd like that, too," he typed.

"In that case, where would you like to go tonight?"

He stared at the words, not sure what to write and wishing he didn't have to key anything. He had wanted to start over and was thrilled to see this wasn't a break-up, but their online chats had long outlived their excitement, ending the moment he had Trisha in his arms for real. And right now, he wanted Trisha in his arms for real.

But taking what he could get, he went along. "I'd like to pull you into my bed and hold you in my arms, kiss those sweet lips and tell you how much I love you."

"That sounds nice. I think I'd like that, too."

"Come here, baby. Settle under the covers and tell me what you're thinking."

A long pause restored his fears and he regretted his earlier actions. He shouldn't have agreed to this meet-ing on the Internet. He should have hopped a plane and followed her to Chicago, so he could see her in person instead of sitting here in the darkness of his den won-dering what was going through her mind.

But the words on the screen relieved the tension.

"I'm thinking I never told you I love you."

A smile broke through his face and he sped his fin-gers over the keyboard. "There are so many things I want to tell you, so many things I want to apologize for. I just wish you were here by my side."

"I wish I was there, too. I miss those warm hands on my thighs, your bare chest against my skin and the feel of your breath against my shoulder."

"I'll do all those things, baby. And I'll do them again when you come home."

From the front room, he heard the doorbell and cursed the interruption. Whoever it was would just have to come back another time.

There was another long pause before the message popped up, "In spirit, I'm always by your side. I always will be."

"When are you coming home? When can we really talk?"

The doorbell rang again and he nearly yelled at the intruder to go away, but another message distracted the thought.

"Don't you think you should answer the door?"

A sharp burst of energy nearly knocked him to the floor and he quickly shoved from the computer and rushed to the entry. Turning the handle, he swung open the door and found Trisha on the doorstep with her laptop at her feet and a wide smile on her flushed, rosy face.

He pulled her into his arms, the chill of her nose stinging his cheek. "You're freezing."

"It was a little colder out there than I expected. I was planning to chat a bit longer, but when you mentioned something about warm covers, I caved."

He held her close, brushing his hands over her arms

to bring back some warmth. "Come in, I'll make you some hot tea."

She smiled, the sparkling gleam in her eyes bringing relief and happiness to his heart. "I'd rather have those warm covers."

It was all the prompting he needed, and in a matter of moments, they'd tossed their clothes and settled together in bed.

Holding her against his chest, he bathed in a long, warm kiss that regenerated his spirit. "I shouldn't have let you go. I shouldn't have ever let you get on that elevator and walk away. And I don't plan to ever make that mistake again."

"Shh," she hushed, pressing her face against his chest. "Let's stop worrying about the past and focus on the future."

He tucked a finger under her chin and lifted her gaze to his. "Okay. I really want to marry you and I really want you back at the agency."

"Yes on the first. No on the second." He opened his mouth to speak, but she pressed a finger to his lips. "I like my job at the bank. The hours are steady, there's less stress and almost no travel. If we're going to have a family some day, one of us needs that stability. Besides, I'm really enjoying working with my mother. She helps me keep things in perspective."

That wasn't the answer he wanted to hear, but he couldn't argue with any of her points. Advertising was a hard business that required a lot of time and travel, and though he wanted Trisha by his side in the office, he liked hearing her talk about family better.

"You don't have to work at the bank to prove anything to me."

"And you don't have to marry me to prove your trust, either." Her smile turned to a grin. "But since you've proposed, I'm not letting you back out now."

He moved his mouth to hers and feasted on those lips he'd forever relish, bringing his hand to one breast and brushing his stiff length against her leg.

He may have lost his best marketing executive, but he'd gained his beloved Scorpio, the woman who had taken his cold, bitter heart and warmed it with her love.

She'd given him his life back, returned the future he thought he'd lost and restored his faith in love and that was worth more than anything she could have given him on the job.

He moved over her and slipped inside, brushing the silky strands of hair from her forehead and pressing his lips to her cheek.

He replied, "Well, if that's the offer on the table, I think we've got a deal."

Epilogue

Daily Horoscope for Libra

It's your birthday! Welcome to the world. Born under the sign of the scales, your life is about balance, and you'll find plenty of that in the years to come. It may not all be bliss, but every rain cloud is followed by bright sunny days and your life will be filled with more than your share.

"SHE'S BEAUTIFUL," Bill announced.

Adrienne's eyes welled with tears. "She looks just like her father."

Logan chuckled. "Don't curse her just yet."

Adrienne's parents looked over the small bundle. "So you decided on the name Summer," her mother said. "I can't think of anything more perfect. She looks like a golden ray of sunshine. I'll have to write a poem to mark the day of her birth."

"Oh, come on, Mom. Trisha doesn't want a poem."

Trisha held her new daughter in her arms, her heart filled with contentment and joy. "Actually, I would love that. Thank you."

"So, when are you going to have the next one?" Adrienne asked, her son, William, asleep in his traveling rocker.

Logan choked. "Let's see if we do a good job with this one, first."

"You'll do fine," Bill assured him. "Kids are a piece of cake."

"You're the ones who should be answering that question," Trisha said. "Will's turning two this month. When are you guys going to take the plunge again?"

Adrienne glanced at Bill. "Well, we didn't want to steal your thunder, but since everyone's here, we might as well let the cat out of the bag."

"You're pregnant?" Adrienne's mother gasped.

She nodded.

"Oh, my God! That's great!" Trisha beamed.

The men shook hands while Adrienne gathered hugs all around, then the group continued to chat and ogle baby Summer until the nurses stepped in and whisked their visitors away.

Logan took a seat on the edge of the bed. "You did good, babe," he said, taking his daughter's tiny hand in his. "She's absolutely perfect."

"Everything's perfect," she said. "I can't imagine my life any better than at this moment."

And it was true. Though her job at the bank kept her busy, it was nowhere near the hectic life she'd had at the agency, and having her mother around on a day-to-day basis made her feel as though she'd truly melded work and family, exactly the way she'd wanted.

Logan and Bill were now full partners, giving both

men more time to spend at home, and after Bill and Adrienne's wedding, the two couples had moved to the suburbs to be closer to family and friends.

It was as if the moment Pisces and Scorpio came together, the planets aligned in their favor, giving weight to the notion that LoveSigns.com knew exactly how to match partners.

With the evening sunset casting a pink glow across the hospital room, Logan pressed a kiss to her lips. "You're right," he agreed. "It doesn't get much better than this."

* * * * *

Happily ever after is just the beginning....

Turn the page for a sneak preview of
A HEARTBEAT AWAY
by
Eleanor Jones

Harlequin Everlasting—Every great love
has a story to tell.™
A brand-new series from Harlequin Books

S pecial? A prickle ran down my neck and my heart started to beat in my ears. Was today really special?

"Tuck in," he ordered.

I turned my attention to the feast that he had spread out on the ground. Thick, home-cooked-ham sandwiches, sausage rolls fresh from the oven and a huge variety of mouthwatering scones and pastries. Hunger pangs took over and I closed my eyes and bit into soft homemade bread.

When we were finally finished, I lay back against the bluebells with a groan, clutching my stomach.

Daniel laughed. "Your eyes are bigger than your stomach," he told me.

I leaned across to deliver a punch to his arm, but he rolled away, and when my fist met fresh air I collapsed in a fit of giggles before relaxing on my back and staring up into the flawless blue sky. We lay like that for quite a while, Daniel and I, side by side in companionable silence, until he stretched out his hand in an arc that encompassed the whole area.

"Don't you think that this is the most beautiful place in the entire world?"

His voice held a passion that echoed my own feelings, and I rose onto my elbow and picked a buttercup to hide the emotion that clogged my throat.

"Roll over onto your back," I urged, prodding him with my forefinger. He obliged with a broad grin, and I reached across to place the yellow flower beneath his chin.

"Now, let us see if you like butter."

When a yellow light shone on the tanned skin below his jaw, I laughed.

"There…you do."

For an instant our eyes met and I had the strangest sense that I was drowning in those honey-brown depths. The scent of bluebells engulfed me. A roaring filled my ears and then, unexpectedly, in one smooth movement Daniel rolled me onto my back and plucked a buttercup of his own.

"And do *you* like butter, Lucy McTavish?" he asked. When he placed the flower against my skin, time stood still.

His long lean body was suspended over mine, pinning me against the grass. Daniel…dear, comfortable, familiar Daniel was suddenly bringing out in me the strangest sensations.

"Do you, Lucy McTavish?" he asked again, his voice low and vibrant.

My eyes flickered toward his, the whisper of a sigh escaped my lips and although a strange lethargy had crept into my limbs, I somehow felt as if all my nerve endings were on fire. He felt it, too—I could see it in his warm brown eyes. And when he lowered his face to mine, it seemed to me the most natural thing in the world.

None of the kisses I had ever experienced could have even begun to prepare me for the feel of Daniel's lips on mine. My entire body floated on a tide of ecstasy that shut out everything but his soft, warm mouth and I knew that this was what I had been waiting for the whole of my life.

"Oh, Lucy." He pulled away to look into my eyes. "Why haven't we done this before?"

Holding his gaze, I gently touched his cheek, then I curled my fingers through the short thick hair at the base of his skull, overwhelmed by the longing to drown again in the sensations that flooded our bodies. And when his long tanned fingers crept across my tingling skin, I knew I could deny him nothing.

* * * * *

*Be sure to look for A HEARTBEAT AWAY,
available February 27, 2007.*

*And look, too, for THE DEPTH OF LOVE
by Margot Early, the story of a couple who must
learn that love comes in many guises—and in
the end it's the only thing that counts.*

This February...

Catch NASCAR Superstar *Carl Edwards* in
SPEED DATING!

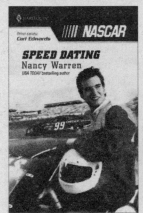

Kendall assesses risk for a living—
so she's the last person you'd
expect to see on the arm of a
race-car driver who thrives on the
unpredictable. But when a bizarre
turn of events—and NASCAR
hotshot Dylan Hargreave—inspire
her to trade in her ever-so-structured
existence for "life in the fast lane"
she starts to feel she might be
on to something!

Collect all 4 debut novels in the Harlequin NASCAR series.

SPEED DATING
by *USA TODAY* bestselling author
Nancy Warren

THUNDERSTRUCK
by Roxanne St. Claire

HEARTS UNDER CAUTION
by Gina Wilkins

DANGER ZONE
by Debra Webb

On sale February 2007

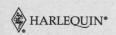

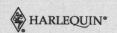

EVERLASTING LOVE™

Every great love has a story to tell™

Save $1.⁰⁰ off

the purchase of
any Harlequin
Everlasting Love novel

Coupon valid from January 1, 2007
until April 30, 2007.

Valid at retail outlets in Canada only.
Limit one coupon per customer.

RETAILER: Harlequin Enterprises Limited will pay the face value of this coupon plus
10.25¢ if submitted by the customer for this product only. Any other use constitutes
fraud. Coupon is nonassignable. Void if taxed, prohibited or restricted by law.
Consumer must pay any government taxes. Void if copied. Nielsen Clearing House
customers submit coupons and proof of sales to: Harlequin Enterprises Ltd. P.O.
Box 3000, Saint John, N.B. E2L 4L3. Non–NCH retailer—for reimbursement submit
coupons and proof of sales directly to: Harlequin Enterprises Ltd., Retail Marketing
Department, 225 Duncan Mill Rd., Don Mills, Ontario M3B 3K9, Canada. Valid in
Canada only. ® is a trademark of Harlequin Enterprises Ltd. Trademarks marked with
® are registered in the United States and/or other countries.

52607370

HECDNCPN0407

HARLEQUIN® *Romance*®

From reader-favorite

MARGARET WAY

Cattle Rancher, Convenient Wife

On sale March 2007.

**"Margaret Way delivers…
vividly written, dramatic stories."**
—*Romantic Times BOOKreviews*

---

*For more wonderful wedding stories,
watch for Patricia Thayer's new miniseries
starting in April 2007.*

Rocky Mountain
BRIDES

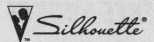

Silhouette®

Romantic
SUSPENSE

Excitement, danger and passion guaranteed!

Same great authors and riveting editorial
you've come to know and love
from Silhouette Intimate Moments.

New York Times
bestselling author
Beverly Barton
is back with the
latest installment
in her popular
miniseries,
The Protectors.
HIS ONLY
OBSESSION
is available
next month from
Silhouette®
Romantic Suspense

Look for it wherever you buy books!

REQUEST YOUR FREE BOOKS!

2 FREE NOVELS PLUS 2 FREE GIFTS!

HARLEQUIN®

Blaze®

Red-hot reads!

HARLEQUIN®

Blaze™

COMING NEXT MONTH

www.eHarlequin.com

HBCNM0207